J-17

Too Hot To Handle

J-17

Love

Too Hot To Handle

by Kate Cann

RED FOX

A Red Fox Book

Published by Random House Children's Books
20 Vauxhall Bridge Road, London SW1V 2SA

A division of Random House UK Ltd
London Melbourne Sydney Auckland
Johannesburg and agencies throughout the world

1 3 5 7 9 10 8 6 4 2

First published in Great Britain by Red Fox 1997

Typeset in Sabon by
Palimpsest Book Production Limited,
Polmont, Stirlingshire

Printed and bound in Great Britain by
Cox & Wyman Ltd, Reading, Berkshire.

Papers used by Random House UK Limited are natural,
recyclable products made from wood grown in sustainable
forests. The manufacturing processes conform to the
environmental regulations of the country of origin.

RANDOM HOUSE UK Limited Reg. No. 954009

ISBN 0 09 925122 1

♥

Anticipation With A Capital A

Free, free, FREE. It was in the air, all around us.
Everyone gathered round in a group, wailing about
the awfulness of the last exam paper, and kissing
and chatting and promising to stay in touch. Then,
shouting 'See you in college!', we all grabbed our stuff
and headed out through the doors.

'No more *school*!' squealed Zoë.

'No more uniform,' I gloated, undoing my tie and
flinging it into a nearby bush.

'We're *adults* now.'

'Too right we are.'

We celebrated by legging it into the newsagents and
buying a huge bag of Fizzy Fish each. Then we went
into the park and hung upside down on the swings and
swung slowly to and fro, letting our hair drag across
the ground. We felt so fantastic it was unreal.

'My brain feels like it's been liquidised,' I said. 'What
we need to do now is some serious relaxing.'

'Mmm – chill out . . .'

I turned to grin at her. 'And think about our holiday
in Greece.'

We both let out a long, blissful sigh. For the last few
weeks, neither of us had allowed even the *thought* of

Greece to enter our scrambled little brains. It would have been like dwelling on steak and chips when you were hooked up to a saline drip feed. But *now* – now we could.

Greece. Blue skies, hot sun, water sports, beach cafés, crystal seas, night life and best of all – fabulous holiday-making *boys*. It was only two weeks away now. We started to discuss it, how it would be, savouring every word, every thought. This was Anticipation with a capital A.

'I can't believe your parents agreed to this holiday,' I said dreamily. 'It is just too brilliant to be real. I mean – it's not really their thing, a flat in Greece, is it?'

'No,' Zoë agreed. 'Dad wanted to do an organised tour round the Scottish castles, complete with hill walking. They get you up 7am, apparently.'

I shrieked with laughter. 'And you changed their minds. You have power, Zoë Chester. Real power.'

She grinned. Zoë has no brothers or sisters, and over the years she's brought her only-child, spoilt-princess act to perfection. She knows just how to use it – like using a weapon. And like a lot of weapons it's really ugly to watch in action but it sure gives results.

When the Chester family annual two-week break came up for discussion, she'd turned her act on full force. 'I feel so *stressed* with these exams,' she'd wailed, wringing her hands and rolling her eyes. 'It would make it all less awful if I had something good to look forward to, something relaxed, somewhere hot.'

They'd bought it. Anything to help the Princess through her exams. A relaxed, hot holiday it was.

♥ 2 ♥

And when she'd said she wanted to bring a friend, they'd bought that too. 'Someone your own age, of course we understand, darling. We know what you girls are like.' Actually, I reckon they wanted a break from the Princess as much as she wanted a break from them.

It caused a few problems, though, because Zoë has *two* friends. Me, and Pandora. Yes, she is really called Pandora, and in my opinion she should never have been let out of her Box.

'Did Pandora really not mind about you taking me to Greece instead of her?' I asked, tipping the last of the Fizzy Fish in my mouth.

'No. Well – not really. Not after I told her it was only fair because you didn't ever get to go away on good holidays.'

'Oh, so I'm a charity case, am I?' I grumbled.

'Oh, don't be sensitive. It worked. I described just how awful your brothers were and how you only ever go on camping holidays and she ended up feeling really sorry for you.'

'How *nice*,' I snarled. 'Anyway, it's not always camping.'

'Yes it is. It has to be because no sane hotel would let you lot through its doors.'

I shoved her backwards onto the grass, but she had a point. I reckon the only way to cope with the horrors of my home is to wear a virtual reality mask permanently clamped to your face. That way it will at least *seem* as if you're somewhere else.

'Come on, Brianna, don't be sour,' said Zoë. 'You

know I'd sooner go with you. You know you're a lot more fun than Pandora.'

'Well, that's not exactly hard,' I said. 'An empty egg box is more fun than Pandora.'

'Oh, shut up. She's OK, really. I promised her I'd send her lots of postcards. So she won't feel left out.'

I laughed. 'Zoë, you won't be able write what we'll be getting up to in Greece on a *postcard*. And if you could – it would make her feel so *completely* left out she'd never speak to you again.'

'Oh, Bri, I hope it's that good,' Zoë said dreamily. 'I really hope so.'

♥
Shop 'Til You Drop

And now – two weeks of glorious anticipation before we went off on the holiday of a lifetime. And two weeks of hard work. Shopping! We had an awful lot to get through. The next day, incredibly early – before 11 am, anyway – we hit the shops, and started the long trawl.

'Brianna, it makes me look *fat*!'

'Nothing makes you look fat. Being *fat* wouldn't make you look fat. Get it.'

'But I like the greeny-blue one, too . . .'

'Get both.'

'Oh – you're right. I mean – beachwear is all-important, right?'

'And nightwear. We should do nightwear next.'

'*Nighties?*'

'No, idiot. Party stuff. Club stuff.'

'Oh, *right*! I think we should go – minimalist.'

At that we both went into high-pitched cackles that got the assistant bearing down on us grimly, asking 'Can I help you?' and meaning 'Shut up or get out.' So Zoë paid for her bikinis and we left the shop.

Shopping that day was pure pleasure. It helped that, for once, we were *loaded*. This was because:

1. we'd been such slaves to revision that our allowances had been left neglected and mounting up in our piggy banks; and
2. both sets of parents had come over all proud and indulgent at all the hard work we'd done and pressed loads of loot on us.

It was great, touring the shops. People getting out of prison must feel just like this. Suddenly everything is there for you again. We ran around, picking stuff up, putting it down, grabbing, trying, buying. It was ace.

'What you've got to remember,' said Zoë as we riffled through a rack of very short, very sheer dresses, 'is just how *incredibly hot* it's going to be.'

'Mmmmm,' I agreed happily.

'I mean – in the day, obviously. But at night too. Those crowded little bars. Clubs, with everyone dancing . . .'

'Pavement cafés under the moonlight . . .'

'I mean – you need to wear the right things.'

'We will,' I said, holding a scrap of purple up against me, 'we will.'

After two hours, we'd bought three short, thin dresses between us. We'd also agreed to swap clothes around on holiday, although I wasn't too sure about letting Zoë wear my new red shift dress.

'It needs my hair to set it off,' I said. 'Your light brown . . .'

'Blonde.'

'It's not.'

'It will be.'

'Oh – OK, then. But I'm wearing it first. Now – nail varnishes.'

I love nail varnish counters – those rows of gorgeous little bright bottles bring out serious greed in me – I want them all, and I can never choose. Luckily, Zoë doesn't have this problem. She grabbed my hand and dobbed some 'Sizzling Cinnamon' on my fingernail.

'H'mm,' she said. 'Hard to tell. I mean – it's a bit too brownish. But it'll look great with *very brown* skin.'

'I'll get it,' I said. 'Now – sun tan lotion.'

By the end of the day we were so weighed down by goodies we could barely walk. 'This is not just indulgence,' Zoë was saying. 'I mean – we're not sad I-shop-therefore-I-am merchants. This is preparation.'

'Yup,' I answered happily. 'Preparation for the best holiday in the history of the world.'

'We have to have some ground rules,' Zoë said as we collapsed exhausted on her bedroom floor. We'd just tried on all the new dresses, swimsuits, bras, makeup and nail varnish we'd bought and had a stand-up fight in the bathroom with some 'scientifically proven' depilatory cream that didn't so much remove the hair on our legs as spread it around a bit.

'Rules?' I moaned. 'Zoë, I never want to hear about another rule as long as I live . . .'

'Some rules are necessary,' said Zoë piously. 'Without them there would be chaos.'

'Great. I love chaos – I worship chaos.'

'Brianna, shut up. Rule 1: no going to bed before 2am.'

'Three am.'

'Rule 2: No reading serious books. Only trash allowed.'

'Agreed!'

'Rule 3: Minimal time spent with my parents.'

'Zoë, that is not a *rule*. That is a requirement for basic *survival*.'

'And Rule 4 – boys.'

'Right! We *have* to get off with at least . . .'

'Brianna! Calm down. This is serious. Holiday romances are . . .'

'*FABULOUS* great wonderful wanna *have one*!'

'Shut *up*, Brianna. Holiday romances are famous for their transitory nature.'

'Y'wha'?'

'They don't last.'

'Yeah – but they're great while they do.'

'Maybe. But the point I'm trying to make *is* – if we *do* have a holiday fling . . .'

'*If*?!'

'. . . we should keep it in perspective. Don't go letting it get all out of hand. Remember boys are just part of the fun. They are *part* of the holiday not the *point* of the holiday. OK?'

'OK,' I said, not really believing it, and we started trying on all our new clothes for the second time.

♥

Organisational Nightmare

Departure Day arrived. I was packed, I had my passport and my purse-load of Greek money, and I was so excited I felt faint. I even felt a bit tearful as I said goodbye to Mum and Dad, and promised to send a postcard express mail as soon as I got there.

Steve, my oldest brother, gave me a lift over to Zoë's house. He usually has to be bribed or bullied into giving me lifts but he has a thing about Zoë and I suppose he thought he'd get another crack at pulling her if he drove me over there.

Some hope. As far as Steve is concerned, Zoë is the original glacial maiden. Her constant rejection just gets him moonier, of course. Boys can be so masochistic.

We drew to a jerky halt outside the Chesters' place, and Steve said, 'I'll see you in, shall I?'

'No need,' I replied firmly, opening my door and clambering out.

'Well, have a great time,' he called after me. 'You lucky cow. God, I wish I was going with you.'

Pulling a face over that horrific thought, I heaved my case out of the boot and staggered up the front path, through the door and smack into Zoë.

We hugged each other, both squealing. Me with excitement, her because I'd dropped my case on her foot.

'Girls, PLEASE!' said a voice. 'Settle down, PLEASE.'

Mr Chester. The only downers to this bliss-trip were Zoë's parents. But as they were also the Organisers, we were stuck.

Organisation – that's the problem. The Chesters organise everything in their lives down to the last tiny detail. They have an antipathy to any kind of spontaneity. And they *worry*. I mean, you'd have thought we were heading for a six year trip to Mars the fuss they were making.

All the cases were lined up in the hall with military precision, and Mr Chester stood over them with his 'last-minute' check list.

'SNORKELS!' he rapped out.

'Blue bag, dear,' Mrs Chester said.

'Anti-diarrhoea tablets.'

'Medical kit, dear. Big suitcase, right hand side.'

And so it went on. He's a dentist, and his approach to everything in life is neat, clinical and preferably with an assistant in attendance, usually Mrs Chester. Or if she's not around, his daughter. So you can't blame Zoë for pulling her appalling Princess act occasionally. It's basic survival.

Mr Chester loaded the cases in the boot, made two final phonecalls, triple-checked the lock-up procedure and the burglar alarm, and we were off. They'd allowed about three hours to get to the airport and it only took forty minutes so Zoë and I had lots of nice hanging around time once we'd got there. Airports are a bit like shopping centres, only with fewer shops and more buzz. I love them.

'Check out the totty in the line,' Zoë hissed, tossing back her newly blonde hair, as we queued up to check in our baggage. 'Anyone on the same flight as us might be with the same Tour company going to the same place.'

'Jeez, I hope not,' I muttered. All I could see ahead of us was a party of shell-suited grannies and two families with about ten whining kids each.

'Eyes behind,' said Zoë, grinning.

Behind us in the queue were about seven lads. Half a footie team. One of them had a ghetto-blaster balanced on his shoulder, blaring out thumping rhythms, and the rest were talking and laughing loudly and moving to the beat.

I swivelled my eyes round and did my best to check them out. And one of them was really special, one of them was . . .

Uh-oh. The music was definitely beginning to get to Mr Chester, and he has a strong sense of citizens' rights. His rights, anyway. He turned towards the boys, frowning.

'Zoë,' I muttered, in panic, 'don't say your dad's going to . . .'

'Would you MIND turning that thing DOWN?' Mr Chester barked, glaring at Ghetto-blaster-boy.

Ghetto-blaster-boy smirked. 'What thing, mate?' he asked.

'You know perfectly well what THING. That

infernal machine you have perched on your shoulder. Why do you imagine the rest of the airport wants to listen to your APPALLING taste in music?'

Zoë had wandered off to stare fixedly in the window of a nearby Knickerbox shop. I joined her. Knickers had never seemed quite so interesting. Meanwhile, Ghetto-blaster-boy had just about worked out that he was being insulted but didn't seem quite sure what to do about it.

'You saying you don't like my music?' he said.

'Oh, you've GRASPED that, have you? Excellent. Now perhaps you'd mind turning it DOWN?'

'On whose orders, mate?' asked one of the bigger ones.

'No one's orders, young man. A polite and civilised REQUEST. That I strongly advise you to FOLLOW.'

A burly uniformed official was heading towards us, attracted by Mr Chester's raised voice. The lads, who had started to edge rather alarmingly towards Zoë's dad, moved back.

'Everything all right, here, sir?' the official asked.

'Perfectly, thank you,' said Mr Chester, smugly. 'These young men were just responding to a request from me to turn their music down.'

'Well done, lads,' said the huge official, swinging round towards them rather like a bull turning on some young goats. The boy with the ghetto-blaster reached up and twiddled with his dial. He would've had to have been made of steel not to.

As everyone moved away, Zoë glared even harder at the window display of knickers and let out a strangled kind of whimper. '*I hate* it when Dad does that. He thinks he's in charge of *everyone*. One day, someone's going to turn on him and *do him over*.'

'Roll on that day,' I thought, as we slunk back to join the Chesters. Mr Chester was smirking in a really irritating way, and saying things to Mrs Chester like, 'A firm hand, you see, Marjorie. All it needs is for a few more people to take a stand against that sort of behaviour and we'd soon have this country back on its feet', and she was agreeing with everything he said. I actually think she was a bit proud of him.

Old couples can be dead weird.

♥

Up, Up And Away

After what felt like months of waiting we were at the head of the queue and checking in our suitcases. Mr Chester only found it necessary to confirm our seating arrangements – two sets of two window seats, non-smoking – three times, and then we headed into the Departure Lounge.

'Well – there's still over an hour to wait until our flight,' said Mr Chester complainingly, as though it wasn't all down to *him* that we'd got to the airport so early.

'Let's go and get a drink, shall we?' said Zoe, brightly. 'I could murder a cappuccino.'

'Cappuccino!' scoffed Mr Chester. 'You two go. Mother and I have bought a flask of tea.' And he sat down on a vacant bench. Mrs Chester pulled a tartan flask from her bag and began pouring. They take flasks everywhere – Mrs Chester hates cafés. That's because two years ago she discovered a lipstick smear on a café cup she was drinking from. Honestly, you'd have thought it was a pair of false teeth clamped to the rim the fuss she made. I know, I was there.

Still, it meant Zoë and I were off the hook. We

escaped gratefully, and found a really sweet little café next to a newsagent's stand.

'Dad does my *head* in,' snapped Zoë. 'I bet those blokes will be on our flight, and that'll be seriously embarrassing.'

'They *knew* we were with him,' I agreed glumly. 'Nobody's that interested in knickers. We were looking in that window for like – half an hour.'

'A couple of them were OK, did you see?' said Zoë, thoughtfully.

'Yes,' I said. 'And they must be going to Rhodes Island if they're on our flight. I really liked the one in the black T-shirt.'

'Didn't notice him,' Zoë lied. Anyone would've noticed him.

'He had brown hair,' I said pointedly. 'And *gorgeous eyes*. And he was tall, and *extremely* fit . . .'

'Boys in a big group are bad news, Brianna,' Zoë broke in, knowledgeably. 'They behave like morons to impress each other.'

'Well – maybe. But they're not going to spend the whole holiday superglued together, are they?'

'Don't you believe it. They're only here to get pissed and go on the pull.'

'Well, aren't we?' I said.

Zoë raised her eyes heavenward. 'Honestly, Brianna, d'you have to be so . . .'

'You're wishing you'd brought Pandora on holiday instead, aren't you?'

Zoë looked at me, grinned, and said 'No way.'

Suddenly, Mrs Chester appeared beside us at the table, looking panic stricken. 'Oh, thank goodness I've found you!' she breathed. 'They've been calling our flight!'

We jumped up guiltily, and ran after her to the departure desk.

'Come ON, girls!' barked Mr Chester. 'It would hardly be an auspicious start to the holiday if we missed the FLIGHT!'

'*God*, I wish we were going away on our own,' hissed Zoë. A group of three very glamorous girls pushed past us, all long legs and expensive haircuts and very much free of adult supervision.

'When we're on the plane let's pretend we're not with your parents,' I whispered back.

'I do that a lot,' replied Zoë, ruefully. 'It doesn't usually work.'

Once on board we edged down the narrow gangway towards our seats. Zoë – typically – grabbed the window seat. Only after I'd told her I didn't care because I expected someone totally lush would take the seat next to me did she promise to swap with me half way through the flight. Some friend.

Mr and Mrs Chester were in the seats in front of us. Mr Chester only made a brief fuss about the overhead locker being too full for his hand luggage, and summoned the air hostess a mere three times to:

1. complain about the proximity of the smoking area;
2. enquire about the exact timing of the serving of lunch; and

3. ask for a pillow for Mrs Chester.

'We're not with them,' said Zoë through gritted teeth. 'We're *not*.'

Then the occupant of the seat next to me arrived – a huge, bald man with too much aftershave on. I pinched Zoë's arm hard to stop her gloating and said, 'I'm holding you to that promise to swap, *friend*.'

Soon we were on our way and we settled down to enjoy the flight. Magazines, boiled sweets to stop our ears popping, bags of honey-sweetened peanuts and a chinking drinks trolley.

'Don't have more than one glass of wine, will you, Zoë dear?' came Mr Chester's voice from the seat in front. 'High altitudes accelerate the effects of alcohol.'

'Sounds great,' grinned Zoë.

Mr Big beside me seemed to think so, too. He'd ordered a succession of brandies, and fallen noisily asleep. And I realised I needed to go to the loo. Badly.

♥

Avoiding Mr Big

There was no way I could squeeze past him. He took up all of his seat, half of my seat and most of the space in front.

'Oh no,' I muttered. 'I'm *desperate*.'

'Wake him up then,' said Zoë calmly.

'I *can't*. He'll go mad.'

'Well, you can't wet the seat,' said Zoë, practically. 'Go on – he'll be asleep again in no time, the amount of booze he's put away.'

So I took a deep breath, and prodded him. Nothing happened, so I shook his arm. Then I said '*excuse me*,' loudly in his ear.

He still slept like the dead.

'I'm going to climb over him,' I announced. 'He's so out of it he won't notice.'

'Oh, *Brianna* . . .' wailed Zoë. '*Don't*!'

As soon as I'd stood up and put one foot on his armrest I regretted it, but I wasn't going to chicken out. I heaved myself up, holding onto the headrest for balance. Slowly, carefully, I reached out across his sleeping form with my other foot and put that on the far armrest. Then I put my other hand on the other side of his head.

It was a dodgy position to be in. I was – to put it bluntly – straddling him. If the plane chose that moment to heave about with turbulence I'd land straight on top of him. I tried to let go and jump sideways, but for some reason I couldn't move.

'*Jump!*' hissed Zoe. 'Brianna – quick! You look like some kind of pervert!'

'I'm . . . I . . . I'm . . .' I whimpered.

'Bri, for heaven's sake *go on*! You'll get arrested! What are you waiting for?'

'I can't!' I wailed. 'I'm *stuck*!'

People had started to turn and look at us. Some of them were laughing, and I could see several disapproving faces. Then I heard: 'They really shouldn't serve so much alcohol on these tourist flights.' I could feel my face getting hotter and hotter, and my limbs getting more and more rigid and unable to move.

Beneath me, Mr Big snored on, breathing brandy up into my face.

'Zoë – help me!' I wailed.

'How?' bleated Zoë, sounding as panicked as I was.

Then a pair of large hands gripped me round the waist, and I heard, 'It's all right, Brianna, I've got you, just let yourself fall towards me.'

I never thought I'd be glad to throw myself into Mr Chester's arms, but I threw myself towards him then as if he was the love of my life.

'Are you all right?' he said sternly, as he set me on my feet in the aisle.

I couldn't even begin to meet his gaze. 'I couldn't

wake that guy,' I said, indicating Mr Big, 'and I *had* to get out . . .'

'Well, get along then,' said Mr Chester.

And I went.

Chronically embarrassing things never happen singly, do they? You never get time to recover from one before the next dumps on you. I rounded the corner to the toilets praying there wasn't a queue – and ran smack into half of the boys from the airport queue.

Apparently they even had to go to the loo in a group.

'Well, look who it is,' said Ghetto-blaster grinning.

I felt myself going bright red. 'Can I get past?' I was *desperate* by this time.

'There's a queue,' said Ghetto-blaster-boy, standing right in front of me.

'Where?'

'Here. We're the queue.'

'Well – that one's empty . . .'

'Is it? You sure?'

If he didn't stop making stupid comments I was going to pee myself. Desperately, I looked behind him, straight at the really gorgeous one.

And he looked back at me.

'Look . . .' I began.

'Oh, stop messing around, Reg,' said the completely gorgeous one, still in riveting eye contact with me. 'Let her through.'

'Get lost, Karl,' Reg laughed. 'Don't you recognise a chat up line when you hear one?'

'Call that a chat-up line?' said Karl, 'You're really sad, mate, you know that?' Then he kind of pushed Reg against the wall, and in the confusion I scrambled into the cubicle, slammed the door shut and locked it. I wasn't planning to come out in a hurry.

♥

Arrival

When I finally emerged from the loo, the lads had gone. Of course I was relieved (in both senses) but I had a good look round for Karl as I swayed back to my seat. He really was a stunner. Shame about his mates. There was no sign of him, though. They must all have been over on the other side of the plane.

When I got back to my seat I found that Mr Big had woken up and was trying to engage a frosty Zoë in conversation.

'Oh, Brianna – hi!' she said, in obvious relief. 'Look – could you let me out, please? I need to . . .'

Mr Big muttered 'Of course, of course' and, after much straining, managed to heave himself out of his chair. Then he let Zoë out, and me in. Smiling, I thanked him – and slid into the window seat.

Well, it *was* my turn.

Another hour, and we arrived. There was a blast of incredible heat as we stepped off the plane and headed into the terminal. There, we collected our luggage, went through passport control, and walked out once again into the wonderful, exotic, scorching heat of Rhodes.

'Oh, my goodness,' whimpered Mrs Chester, fanning herself frantically. 'Oh, my *goodness*. Oh, this is dreadful.'

'Now, Marjorie,' said Mr Chester soothingly. 'You will acclimatise, you know.'

'Oh, I won't,' she wailed. 'Not to this. Oh, it's *awful*!'

A plump, official-looking tour rep bustled over, obviously fully trained in the art of spotting potential panic-situations.

'Chester party?' she said brightly. 'This is your coach – it's fully air conditioned.'

Mrs Chester's feet barely touched the ground as Mr Chester propelled her towards the coach. Zoë and I were picking up two suitcases to follow when we heard uproar behind us. We swivelled round to look. It was the lads from the plane, going crazy with excitement from the sudden blast of heat. As one, they dropped their bags and began ripping off their T-shirts.

'God, and they say *we're* the vain sex,' muttered Zoë, staring hard. 'They can't bear to waste a second's tanning time.'

I was trying to look indifferent while I craned frantically to see Karl. He always seemed to be behind the others.

'Stuart party?' called the tour rep, heading towards them.

'Yep! That's us!' Reg shouted. 'Let's go, guys!'

♥ 23 ♥

'This coach,' she said, indicating ours. 'And look lads – I don't want sweat all over my seat backs. Put your T-shirts back on.'

'Spoilsport,' hissed Zoë, then we turned and hurried onto the coach ahead of them.

Mr Chester waved to us from a seat near the back so we more or less had to go and join him. The boys got on and filled up the seats at the front. I suppose the last thing they wanted to do was sit near Mr Chester.

Soon we were off, driving through sun-bleached countryside. Fig trees and cactus plants grew by the roadside, with goats grazing in among them. It was all so different from home I felt shivery with excitement. And when I wasn't staring out of the window, I was staring at the back of Karl's head. He'd looked round at me a couple of times when the journey had started, but that was it. I felt quite disappointed until I realised he'd fallen asleep. Most of his mates had, too. They were all sagging at the necks and sprawling into the aisle.

'Too much lager on the plane,' snorted Mr Chester.

The tour rep picked up a microphone and began to lecture us on avoiding mosquitoes and not getting sunburned. Every now and then, the coach would stop and she'd escort a few people off and into their holiday flats, then come trotting back.

Then we stopped outside a line of huge concrete tower-block hotels, and she announced, 'Faliraki!' And the lads all came to, dragged their bags off the racks and staggered off the coach. As they left, Ghetto-blaster-boy turned round and shouted, 'See ya girls!'

Mr Chester snorted, again. He had an amazing repertoire of snorts. 'Thank goodness we won't be seeing those louts again,' he said.

Lindos was the last stop, and I noticed with interest that it wasn't that far from Faliraki. We dismounted, and the tour rep explained we'd have to walk to the apartment and the cases would be delivered by motorbike-pulled trailer later on. No cars were allowed in the ancient centre of Lindos. Mainly because they wouldn't fit.

We started to follow her into the tiny town, along the steep, narrow lanes, past the gleaming white houses. Zoë and I had gone all giggly with excitement. The sun was just starting to set and this strange, hot wind was blowing – it felt like a jacuzzi with air instead of water.

As we got closer to the centre, the streets got more crowded. There were groups of people with lilos and beach-bags staggering back late from the beach, and groups of early-evening revellers, all dolled up, heading for the bars. In among the seriously glamorous people were some great-looking lads, unfortunately all with girls velcroed to their sides. We wove our way through everyone, trying not to feel intimidated, trying to look relaxed.

'Oh, this is *brilliant*!' said Zoë at my side. 'It's like – so *exotic*.'

'Don't you feel really – "first day here", though?' I murmured.

'Yes,' she agreed. 'And incredibly *white*.'

'In a couple of days,' I whispered, 'we'll have this place sussed. It's going to be ace.'

We stared into seductive looking bars and tiny shops full of souvenirs as we passed. Old ladies in black sitting outside the shops stared back.

Mr and Mrs Chester were looking grim faced. 'Have you seen the pictures on some of those T-shirts?' peeped Mrs Chester, pointing to the lines strung between the shops like washing.

'Pornographic!' growled Mr Chester. 'Keep up, girls!'

'Here we are!' said the tour rep, coming to a stop beside a flight of worn stone steps. 'This is one of my favourite apartments. It's very old.'

'Oh, dear,' murmured Mrs Chester.

We followed the rep up the steps and she opened a dark wooden door, like the door to a chapel. Then we were inside, only we were still outside. The late sun streamed down on us, and a soft wind blew.

'This is the terrace,' said the rep. 'The rooms all lead off this.'

The terrace was crammed with masses of lush plants. Some grew tall against the walls, some tumbled out of their pots across the ground; all dripped and sparkled from a recent watering. A thick vine canopy swayed above a table and four chairs. Along the open side of the terrace ran a low stone wall; beyond it, in the distance, you could see the sea.

'It's *fabulous*!' breathed Zoë, eyes huge.

'*Wonderful*,' I added fervently.

It was a dream place. But you could tell Mrs Chester was having enormous difficulty getting her head around a room that didn't have a ceiling over it. Or curtains.

'Is there a living room?' she asked faintly.

'Well, this is it,' said the rep. 'Bit hot in the day, but then everywhere is, isn't it? That vine gives a good shade, though. Just watch the bugs don't fall in your gazpacho!'

'Can I see the bedrooms?' Mrs Chester said, fainter still.

As the rep showed her towards the main bedroom, Zoë and I dashed into the other one. It was great. One window, onto the terrace; two plain beds, all crisp cotton sheets; white washed walls, a washbasin and a cool, tiled floor.

'Which bed d'you want?' Zoë asked.

'You're giving me first choice?' I said, amazed.

'No, but if you don't want mine, we won't have to fight, will we?'

'Typical. Well, I like being near the door.'

'Great! I don't. Now – how big's the wardrobe?' She wrenched the door open. 'Brilliant. Huge. And look – that stone windowsill. Perfect makeup station.'

Laughing excitedly, we began to unpack, hanging up all our gorgeous new clothes, laying out our gear. Then there was a thin wail from outside: 'De – rek! There's no *shower* curtain!'

Giggling, we pushed past a stricken-looking Mrs

Chester into the bathroom. It was a plain, tiled cell with a shower hose on the wall, a basin and a loo.

'It's great!' said Zoë. 'No one can tell me off for flooding the floor.' She pointed to the central drain. 'You're *meant* to flood it.'

Mrs Chester had moved into the kitchen. 'I'll never be able to cook proper meals in that oven,' she said, piteously.

'Oh, Mum,' said Zoë. 'You're on holiday. You're not supposed to *cook*. We can eat out. There're loads of little bistros and bars and places.'

'Well, your father won't like that. Not every night. He likes a proper dinner.' And she started to unpack a bag she'd brought. It was full of packets of tea and All Bran and J-cloths and disinfectant.

'How depressing,' murmured Zoë, and we escaped.

Mr Chester was seated at the terrace table, determinedly opening the complementary bottle of wine. 'Drink, girls?' he said. 'First night of the holiday, after all. Then I thought we'd go out to eat. The tour representative recommended a fish restaurant down on the local beach.'

'Blimey, what's got into him?' muttered Zoë.

'He's decided to have a good time,' I answered. 'Let's get ready!'

♥

Newbies

We swapped our flight-worn gear for shorts and T-shirts – no point wearing the good stuff until we'd got the tans to go with it – and followed Mr and Mrs Chester down the steep path to the beach.

'As soon as we get our bearings, we'll ditch them,' whispered Zoë. 'But right now I'm starving.'

The restaurant was under a huge, coloured canopy; sand from the beach drifted across the sun-bleached planks of its floor. It was buzzing with life. Waiters carrying bottles and plates of seafood whirled between tables packed with brown, confident people.

'Cross your fingers,' hissed Zoë.

'Hoping what?'

'That Dad doesn't completely embarrass us.'

I crossed them on both hands.

Mr Chester strode into the centre of the restaurant and looked around him challengingly. A dark-haired waitress approached us. 'Do you speak English?' he demanded.

'Yes, love,' she replied. 'I'm from Bradford.'

'Ah. Well – a table for four, please. Next to the beach if possible, and on the left side.' He turned to

Mrs Chester. 'They're furthest from the toilets, dear,' he explained.

Cringing, Zoë and I followed him to our table. I knew Zoë was a bit in awe of everything, a bit unsure, just like me. But it would have been taboo to discuss it. What we had to do now was keep a low profile, and watch what was going on, and in a few days – well, we'd really be on holiday then.

Mr Chester laid down his menu. 'Full Seafood Platter for me,' he pronounced. 'After all, when in Rome, do as the Romans do. Or in this case, when in Greece, do as the Grecians do, eh? Ha, ha.'

And Mrs Chester actually laughed with him. 'You're brave, Derek,' she peeped. 'Just pasta for me. I don't want a funny tummy.'

'I'd like pizza,' Zoë muttered.

'Me too, please,' I said.

'Oh, you girls. So unadventurous, eh?' Mr Chester smirked.

Once we'd ordered, the waitress brought the drinks and cutlery. She laid out a whole array of instruments by Mr Chester's plate, and he picked them up one by one and examined them, smiling. It was like he was back in his dental surgery again.

When the food arrived, I could hardly bear to watch him in action. He kept this running commentary up, too. 'Ah, this is efficient. You hold the shell SO – and then you prise the flesh out with this – and then . . .'

'*Dad*,' broke in Zoë. 'We're finished. We're going for a stroll along the beach, OK?'

Mr and Mrs Chester exchanged glances. 'OK,' Mr Chester said. 'But not too far.'

We got to our feet thankfully.

'Sure you don't want a pudding?' he bellowed, as we wove our way through the tables. 'Watching those waistlines, are we?'

It was a relief to escape onto the dark beach. As we walked away from the bright lights of the restaurant, we could hear the waves, loud and rhythmic, in front of us. We reached the shoreline and sat side by side, throwing pebbles into the water.

'It's still so *hot*,' murmured Zoë.

'That sea looks wonderful,' I said. 'I can't wait to get in it.'

Zoë looked at me, grinning, and I looked back, and then we both looked all around us, to see if there was anyone nearby. Then we stripped down to our underwear and ran into the water.

We splashed and swam around blissfully in the warm waves, then floated on our backs and looked up at the sky and its amazing stars, until Zoë started banging on about squids and jellyfish, so we both ran out, shrieking.

'Wurr,' Zoë grumbled. 'Not so warm now!'

'And we've got no towels.'

'Never mind. Shake it off. Oh, Bri – look!'

A little blunt head was looking over the top of one of Zoë's sandals. It watched us for a second, then with a whisk of green tail, it was gone.

'A lizard!' said Zoë, in such awe that we both laughed.

We walked back to the restaurant to meet the Chesters, and Zoë bought a couple of postcards from a stand there. Then, when we got back to our room, I scribbled a postcard to Mum and Dad to tell them I was fine, and Zoë wrote to Pandora. She wondered aloud about me signing it too, but we thought that would be a bit tactless.

Hi Pandora! Well, we're here! The apartment is really sweet, and right near the beach. Mum and Dad are being **pitiful** as usual, but Brianna and I don't plan to spend too much time around them. Want to get some serious tanning in over the next few days because I KNOW the tan you bring back from Nice is going to be **fantastic**! Lotsa love, Zoë xxx

Greek-God Watch

We were woken early next day by shouting and clattering from the street outside. We ran to lean over the wall, and stood staring down at a line of donkeys, each with a tourist astride.

'Poor *things*,' muttered Zoë. 'Look at that guy on the little brown one – he must weigh fifteen stone!'

I cupped my hands to my mouth like a loudhailer and boomed, 'WALK – you lazy scumbags! Get off and WALK!' Then we both dropped giggling out of sight behind the wall.

'What are you girls up to?' said Mrs Chester, emerging from the kitchen. 'Come on – breakfast's ready.'

'Oh, *Mum*,' wailed Zoë. '*Muffins*? This is *Greece*!'

'I don't care,' said Mrs Chester stubbornly. 'You still need a good breakfast inside you. And I'm packing up a picnic for the beach.'

'Oh, terrific,' groaned Zoë, as we both grabbed a muffin and went to get ready.

We followed the Chesters down to the beach, pretending we weren't with them. Mr Chester was carrying about six bags, three lilos and two sun umbrellas, and he was wearing this little beanie hat that was too naff to be true. Then, when we got there, we found you had to *hire* the sunbeds and umbrellas, so most of his stuff wasn't needed anyway.

'Now – you be VERY careful in the sun at first,' he lectured us loudly as we peeled off. 'Lots of cream. You don't want to burn on your FIRST DAY.'

'Does he have to point out to *every single person* on the beach how *white* we are?' snarled Zoë, as we spread cream on our legs.

'Just – ignore him. Come on – fifteen minutes each side, then let's go for a swim.'

As we settled back on our sunbeds, we noticed something. Just about everyone else who was sunbathing was doing it bareback. I mean everyone.

'Jesus,' muttered Zoë, looking round. Girls were strolling along the beach topless, playing in the waves topless, sitting and chatting to *men* topless. Mrs Chester took off her robe to reveal a huge floral costume with serious bust underpinning, and sat there looking scandalised. Mr Chester sat next to her very obviously *not* looking at anyone.

'No way,' said Zoë, shaking her head in disbelief. 'No *way*.' And – for the moment at least – I agreed.

We lay down and let the sun flay us. It was easy remembering all the warnings about the dangers of sunburn. That heat felt savage. It was only good for a very short time.

It's weird, switching to beach mode. You have to get used to functioning with barely any clothes on, and you have to get used to that laid-back, loping style of walking along the sand. But as the day gradually unwound, so did we. Once we'd been in the sea a couple of times, and sussed out how to use the freshwater shower by the café, and bought a couple of ice-creams using real, Greek money – we felt we belonged.

'Bri, do you notice anything depressing about this beach?' asked Zoë, as we lay down for another spot of sun-worshipping.

'Everyone has bigger tits than us?'

'That's not true! No – the good-looking guys are all with girls.'

'I know. Just like last night.'

There was a couple a metre or so away from us who were so in love it made you ill just to watch them, but you found yourself watching them all the same. They kept rubbing oil over each other, and stopping to smooch. Then they'd prance out into the waves and play this pat-ball game with little bats and a ball. Then they'd come back in and rub in more oil and have another torrid smooch.

'I reckon it's honeymoon beach, Brianna,' said Zoë, glumly.

'Well . . .' I began, 'it's not the *only* beach on the island . . .' and I was just about to launch into my little plan for a day-trip out to Faliraki in search of Karl when she jabbed me with her elbow, hard.

Two guys were sauntering along towards us, just where the sea met the sand. They were both tall, and slim, and very tanned. They had their heads tipped back and these very, very expensive shades on.

They caused a distinct ripple as they walked by. Even Ms Totally in Love nearby had a quick lech before going back to massaging loverboy's shoulders.

'Forget it, Zoë,' I hissed.

'Your problem, Brianna,' she hissed back, 'is that you always set your sights too low.'

We watched them promenade in slow motion to the end of the beach, then swing round and start back again. They exuded this incredible elegance, and this scary, but altogether desirable, confidence. Unlike most blokes, they had no need to show off. Just being what they were was enough.

'Stop drooling, Zoë,' I whispered. 'It doesn't look nice.'

'Shut up. Oh, *God*, they're gorgeous.'

And then the miracle happened. They stopped right near us, and began wading slowly out to sea.

'Let's go for a swim!' I said brightly.

'You are so *obvious*!' snapped Zoë. 'Wait!'

We watched as their beautiful brown backs slowly sank from sight, and they began swimming. Then, as casually as we could, we set out after them.

They were doing a type of lazy breast stroke out to the rocks at the side of the bay, barely splashing their sun-specs. When they reached the rocks they clambered out onto them. For a few moments, they were stunningly framed against the blinding, blue sky. Then one of them took off his sunglasses, put them down, stepped to the edge of the rock, and dived in.

'Ooo – oooh!' gurgled Zoë. 'Serious heroics!'

We were both frantically treading water, so we could stay in the best ogling spot. We watched as Greek God Number Two stepped to the edge and dived. He actually flipped up into the air for a second, before coming down and entering the water like a spear.

'Ooo – oooh!' moaned Zoë again. She has an exaggerated respect for male physical prowess. To be honest I'm not exactly indifferent to it myself.

We watched them climb out and dive in two more times before we felt we really had to swim off – we were beginning to look too obvious. No one treads water for that long, even if they are having the kind of animated conversation that we were faking at the time. We swam slowly back to the beach, trying to decide which of the two was the most fantastic and discussing how things on the beach scene had taken a clear turn for the better.

When we got back to shore, things improved even more. Mr Chester was standing there, all packed up. 'Mother's not feeling too good,' he said to Zoë. 'She's had enough of this heat. I thought we'd take the picnic back up to the apartment, and then maybe we can all have a little nap.'

Woooow. Exciting.

'Oh, Dad,' said Zoë. 'We love it here. You go on, and we'll meet you later.'

'But what about your lunch? Mother's made some lovely egg sandwiches. Look – I'll get yours out . . .'

Zoë put a hand on his arm. 'Don't Dad. They'll spoil in the heat. We'll grab something at one of these cafés, and then have the sarnies later, eh?'

Mr Chester looked resigned. 'Have you got enough money?' he said. 'Here – take this.' And he handed a couple of notes to Zoë. Then the Chesters tottered off and we were on our own. Parentless at last.

♥

Classy Guys!

The first thing we did was go and buy two flimsy sarong cover-ups. We'd sussed that these were what you put on when you went to get lunch. You tied them round your waist and they kind of floated round you, not really covering you up at all, but making you look all gone-native and sexy. Then we toured the outside of all the cafés, checking the menus and (more importantly) the clientele.

'Come on, Zoë,' I moaned. 'This is the third time we've schlepped along here. Let's *choose*.'

'Oh, OK. Well – those two guys aren't in any of them. That first one has three blokes on their own but crap food. This one has the best – *ambience*.'

'Y'wha?'

'Ambience, you peasant. You know – atmosphere. And that one has a lot of life but a lot of couples.'

Finally, after more discussion, we settled on the last one. Truth was, we were a bit scared about going in on our own. This wasn't exactly Pizza Hut on the High Street any more. I made Zoë promise to do the ordering and she kept checking with me how many drachmas there were to the pound. Then we went in.

It was really lively inside. Zoë ordered two Cokes at the bar and we asked for a table. Then we sat down, trying not to look all excited, as though we'd pulled off something big.

'Don't have pizza,' Zoe hissed at me. 'Have shellfish.'

'But I hate shellfish!'

'I don't care. It's cool.'

'I won't look cool if I start gagging on it. I'm having a baguette. Avocado and bacon. Yum.'

'Oh – OK,' she agreed, sulkily, as the waiter appeared beside us.

'Two lovely ladies all alone?' he gushed mechanically. No, I thought, we're with each other.

'What can I get you?' he went on.

We ordered, and relaxed back, gazing about us.

'This is *great*,' said Zoë. 'I love eating with hardly any clothes on. D'you think I'm getting brown already?' We both gazed mutely down at the pink forearm she'd shoved forward.

'Give it another few days, Zoë, you can't expect . . .' then I broke off and gawped at the bar. The guys had come in. I mean – The Guys.

'Oh, *wow*,' I hissed. 'D'you reckon they saw us come in here?'

Zoë had gone kind of rigid, like a pointer dog when it spots a duck in the reeds. 'Go and get some more *drinks*,' she murmured.

'Me?' I wailed, softly. 'You go. You're the sophisticated one.'

'Yeah, but you're the funny one. Go on Brianna

– it's your *turn*.' And she kicked me hard under the table.

As casually as I could, I stood up, briefly rearranged my cutlery and sauntered over to the bar. As I got there, the guys were just being served. I stood close enough to them to be noticed, but not enough to look obvious, and waved my drachmas at the barman.

'What's the food like here?' came a voice to my left. Oh, this was too good to be *true*. One of them was *talking* to me.

'Er – OK, I think. I mean – we've not eaten yet. But it looks OK.'

Killer. Why do I always witter like that?

The barman whirled across to take my order, and while I gave it I racked my brains for a way of continuing the conversation. But there was no need.

'So – on holiday?' the voice said, which was a monumentally stupid remark to make, but I reacted with as much delighted surprise as if he'd just guessed my name, age and telephone number.

'Well – *yeah*! Yeah, we are! You?'

'Yes. Just a short break. We're off to do the Inca Trail next. In the Andes. You know, Peru. We wanted a few days relaxing in the sun first.'

I made myself turn to look at him, hanging onto the bar in case his sheer gorgeousness caused my legs to give way. 'Wow!' I bleated, not really knowing what I was saying. 'The Inca Trail! You must be so *fit*!'

Fit – I actually called him fit! AAGH! Great, Brianna, just great.

But he was laughing suggestively. 'Well – thank

you. Hey – if you haven't eaten yet, why don't we join you? That's your friend over there, isn't it? At a table for four?'

Oh, this was so smooth it was scary. Some demon was going to pop up any minute now and demand my soul if I wanted this scene to continue. I choked out, 'Sure – great – why not . . .' picked up our drinks, and headed over.

Zoë is some actress. I mean, someone really should give her an Oscar. As we walked over she pretended to be studying the menu, and then she looked up all cool, and said, 'Hi?' slightly frostily, as though she was marginally miffed at having her girly lunch interrupted.

'Hi,' came the reply. 'I'm Jason, and this is Mark. OK if we join you for lunch? Your friend just invited us.' Which wasn't exactly true and also made me sound like a right pushy tart, but never mind.

Zoë waved a languid hand. 'Sure. Help yourselves.'

And they did.

It was weird having these two icons sitting opposite. Unreal. They looked so polished, so perfect – everybody's ideal holiday romance.

The conversation that followed was smooth as olive oil – on Mark and Jason's part, anyway. They told us about the island, where the best beaches were, and what other parts of it were worth visiting. It turned out Jason's folks owned a 'little house' in Lindos, so they came here quite a lot.

'Have you been into old Lindos at night yet?' asked Mark.

'No,' replied Zoë. 'We've only just got here. It looks great though.'

'Oh, it *used* to be great,' said Jason. 'But it's got so tacky and commercial over the years. Half the restaurants serve up pizza and chips now. Still, there are a few good places left if you know how to find them.' Then he leaned dizzyingly across the table towards me. 'Maybe we could show you one or two.'

I left the reply to Zoë, because my throat seemed to have seized up. 'Oh, that would be lovely,' she said calmly. 'It did all look a little – confusing.'

'Are you booked up tonight?'

'No – no we're not. We were just going to wander around, take a look, you know . . .'

'Well, why don't we meet you? And then we can all eat together. I know a fantastic seafood restaurant.'

'That would be great,' said Zoë. 'We adore seafood.'

They found out where our apartment was, and said they'd call for us at eight. Then Jason beckoned to the waiter for the bill. 'This is on us, girls,' he said.

'Oh, we couldn't . . .' began Zoe:.

'Sure you could.' He chucked some plastic down, and we stood up to go.

When we got outside I was hoping we'd all go and sunbathe and swim together, but Jason and Mark said they had something on that afternoon. 'You enjoy the rest of the day,' said Mark. 'And we'll see you at eight. Don't get sunburned, OK?' Then they sauntered off.

Zoë and I headed for our sunbeds. We were both nearly passing out with excitement.

'I can't *believe* how easy that was,' squeaked Zoë. 'They even paid for lunch.'

'This place must be enchanted,' I said moonily. 'Where dreams come true. We were handed them on a *plate*.'

'Which one d'you like best? Come on, Bri, tell me.'

'Not sure. Mark, I think. Or maybe – well, they're sort of similar, aren't they?'

'Both absolutely fabulous.'

'That Jason bloke must be seriously loaded,' I added.

'I know. I felt a bit – I mean, those guys seemed to know it *all*. I had a chronic inadequacy attack during lunch.'

'Zoë – you didn't find them a bit – stuck up, did you?'

'All that stuff about Lindos going downhill? Dunno. They've probably got a point.'

'Anyway, who cares. We're only on the second day of our holiday and we're going out tonight with two of the classiest lads on the island!' And we both lurched into the sea, splashing like maniacs.

♥

Leave Dad To Me...

We decided to leave the beach quite early that day, while the late afternoon sun was still hot. We had to put in some serious glamorisation time. As we plodded up the hill to the apartment, a sudden awful thought hit me. 'Zoë,' I squeaked, 'how are you going to handle your dad? I mean – what's he going to think? We've picked up a couple of blokes on the beach and we're meeting them tonight?'

'Well – that's what's happened,' she said, calmly.

'Yes, but he'll –'

'Oh, leave him to me. Don't worry about it, Brianna.'

So I didn't. As soon as we got in I headed for the shower. It's lovely, feeling all the sand and sea-salt wash away, and your skin just a little bit sore from the sun – then you lather in gallons of moisturiser to repair any damage. We both had distinct marks where our cozzies stopped, which we compared jealously.

It took us only half an hour to agree which clothes we'd wear. We had to get the right balance between looking completely wonderful and not trying too hard. Then we moved on to hair, makeup, nails . . .

'What about your egg sandwiches, dears?' called Mrs Chester from the terrace.

Zoë pulled a face. But I was hungry. For some reason, I'd only been able to swallow half my lunch. 'It's a good idea to line your stomach,' I explained, as I left the room. 'Come on – and you'd better tell your dad what we're doing tonight.'

I leaned up against the terrace wall, chewing egg sarnie, listening to Zoë explain. What a con artist. It was an education just to listen to her. She didn't lie outright, but she knew just which bits to embellish to convince Mr Chester that what we were up to was fine, even educational. She said that Mark and Jason knew all about the island, and might take us sightseeing later on (go for it, Zoë!), and we were meeting them tonight to go to a restaurant 'that a friend of Jason's father runs'. The final decider was the fact that the lads were coming here to pick us up. I'd hoped to avoid them meeting the Chesters – to maybe dash outside when we saw them coming – but I trusted Zoë's instinct to know what was needed.

Then we went back to our room to carry on getting ready. I redid my nails, while Zoë tried to lecture me on how to act that evening. She seemed really wound up about it. When I told her to get lost, she stomped out to the terrace with her writing things.

Dear Pandora & Droolsome news. We have met two of the most amazing lads! They're about twenty, and so cool, so laid back - seriously sophisticated! We're going out to eat with them tonight. I just can't believe it. I hope this is IT for the holiday. I just hope Brianna doesn't BLOW IT! Wish YOU were here ♡ Zoë xx

Mark and Jason turned up at 8.05 pm, and were so unbelievably charming to Mrs Chester that she practically asked them to forget the restaurant and stay on to dinner. As it was, we all had sparkling wine and cashew nuts forced on us while Mr Chester cross-examined the lads.

'Now I'm trusting you two young men to get the girls back no later than midnight, all right?' said Mr Chester in a jovial, men-together way as we inched our way to the door.

'Oh, absolutely, Mr Chester,' said Jason. 'No problem.'

'*Sorry* about Dad,' Zoë blurted, as we went down the steps.

'Why? He's just protective,' answered Mark urbanely. 'So shall I be, when I have daughters.'

Together, we strolled into the centre of Lindos. What a glam group we must look, I thought, proudly. I just wished I could think of something to say.

Zoë was stricken with the same silence affliction. But Jason and Mark didn't seem bothered. They kept up a running commentary as we wandered along, which bar did the best cocktails, which restaurant brought in the best profit, who was running which scam. Then we stopped outside an exclusive-looking little place with wrought iron bars at the windows, and Jason began to speak to the doorman.

In Greek.

Those two were so suave, it was unreal. I was feeling completely out of my depth by this time, and I knew Zoë was too, although she'd have had her toenails pulled out before admitting it.

Within minutes we'd been whisked inside to a table in the corner, half-hidden by an enormous potted palm, and leather-bound menus had been placed in our hands.

'Well, girls, what's it going to be?' asked Mark. 'I'm having the lobster. It's excellent here.'

Zoë asked for braised swordfish, while I scanned the menu in desperation. 'I'll have the kalimari,' I said, wildly.

Then the wine waiter came over, and Mark and Jason got stuck into a deep conversation with him, all about vintages and stuff.

'D'you know what kalimari is?' Zoë hissed at me.

'No – what?'

'Squid.'

'Oh, Jesus.' I could feel myself going green already, and the plate hadn't been put in front of me yet. I'll relax soon, I told myself, as the waiter filled our glasses and the starters arrived. This is amazing, being here with them. This is what a holiday is all about.

Then Mark and Jason started to talk about their Andean trek. They went into great detail about the route they planned to take, stopping for a brief argument about whether to take the longer trail all the way up to the mountains, despite the freezing conditions at night. They told us all about how perilous the Dead Women's Pass (*great* name) was going to be, and, by implication, how brave they were to tackle it. They recounted in exact detail the training they'd been putting in over the last six months, to bring them to their obvious present peak of physical fitness.

After a while, Zoë and I gave up making little admiring noises and asking little interested questions, but it didn't put them off their stride. They worked out in front of us how they would keep a check on average mileage per day, and how much allowance they would make for weather and altitude. They practically gave us an inventory of the gear they were taking along with them, and then spent a good ten minutes discussing the relative virtues of each others' trekking boots.

It was all so disappointing. Mark and Jason made being boring into an art form. They droned on through both courses and up until the waiter wheeled the dessert trolley over to us. I hadn't enjoyed the meal one bit, and not mainly because I'd had to eat wriggly disgusting squid tentacles, either. Mark and Jason were so up themselves it was appalling. I'd even stopped fancying them.

'No one keen on dessert?' murmured Mark. 'Why don't we wander back to the house for coffee? I'd love you to see it – it has a stunning view of the Acropolis.'

I wished Zoë and I had had the guts to behave like complete girlies and gone to the bog together. That way we could've worked out a tactful way to escape. But we didn't so we found ourselves towed along the crowded streets and up the steps to their 'little house'.

Everything ran as smoothly as clockwork once we were inside – it was sinister. The wine was chilling, the smoochy music all lined up, the door to the balcony open. Mark invited Zoë out to 'look at the view', and as soon as they'd gone, Jason put his arms round me, and steered me towards the spiral staircase.

'Let's leave them alone,' he whispered.

I pushed him away. There was no way I even wanted to *kiss* him, at this stage. 'I wouldn't mind seeing the view from the balcony myself,' I said, stalling.

'Oh, but four's a crowd, don't you think?' he said, and put his arms round me again.

'Look,' I said, disentangling myself. 'This is – ridiculous. What did you do – draw lots to see who

♥ 49 ♥

ended up with who? I mean – it's not as though we've made any sort of – connection together.'

'Well,' he murmured, like some phoney film character, 'that's what I'd like to put right, Zo – Brianna.'

'You *see*!' I squawked in triumph. 'You nearly got my name wrong. I'm out of here. Thanks for the dinner and everything, but no thanks.'

Zoë appeared at the door to the living room, looking pink. 'You coming, Brianna?' she choked out. And we fled into the night.

♥

Beach Vampires

Outside, we had a fit of hysterical giggles.

'What a pair of *creeps*,' I shrieked.

'They thought they could bore us half to death . . .'

'And then get off with us!'

'On the balcony – I felt I was being watched by a lizard – a real reptile.'

'Urgh – the mechanical men. Urgh, they were revolting.'

'They must try it on with every girl they meet. Same old routine. That's why it felt so – *tired*.'

'They didn't want to talk to us. They didn't really like us. They didn't really *see* us.'

'They're beach vampires,' Zoë said, inspired. 'Attracted by our white skin. That meant we were new and out of our depth and . . .'

'Easy prey.'

'Yeah. And you know what was the most insulting bit of all?'

'What?' I asked.

'That they didn't try very hard. I mean – they couldn't even be bothered to *talk* to us properly. They didn't really care one way or the other.'

'Creeps,' I agreed.

'Patronising gits,' she added.

'Boring, boring jerks.'

'Stuck-up sleazebags.'

This heartfelt exchange went on for quite a while. It really made us feel better, as we hurried through the narrow lanes.

Then, after a while, it dawned on us that we weren't exactly sure where we were hurrying *to*. In fact, we were lost.

'Oh, save us' muttered Zoe, checking her watch. 'It's ten to twelve. We'll get the "If-I-can't-trust-you-to-get-back-on-time-how-can-I-trust-you-out-so-late-and-in-a-foreign-country-too" routine.'

'Zoë, I'm beginning to feel worried about getting back *at all*, never mind late. All these streets look the same. It's like a maze.'

'I'm sure it was this way. Down here, past this church.'

'Wurgh. It looks all dark and spooky along there.'

'But I'm sure it leads into – *AAAAAGH!*'

A figure draped from head to foot in black cloth had stepped out in front of us, blocking the path. I was about to echo Zoë's scream when I realised it was a priest.

'Holiday maker?' he said, in a thick Greek accent.

'Y-yes,' I stuttered.

'I know. Santa Maria. You lost?'

'Y-yes,' Zoë admitted.

'Follow me.'

'Santa Maria,' whispered Zoë. 'That's what our

apartment's called. He must be going to take us there.'

'Either that or lock us up in a nunnery,' I muttered, as we started off after him. We followed the trailing black cloak further into the dark maze of streets, recognising none of them. But within five minutes, we were heaving a joint sigh of relief on the familiar steps outside our apartment. The priest pointed to the tiny chapel opposite. 'Mine,' he said simply, then he bowed and glided silently away.

'Thank you *so* much,' gushed Zoë after him. Then she carried on loudly: 'Wonderful evening – it was really great! Bye, Jason – Bye, Mark! Thanks! Byeee!'

'What,' I snorted, as we ran up the steps, 'was all *that* about?'

'No point letting the 'rents know how it all turned out,' she muttered.

The following day, we were both rather subdued when we crawled out of bed. Mr Chester wanted to try out St Paul's Bay beach, which he said was very quiet and secluded. Normally, of course, we would have been dead against anything quiet or secluded, but today it suited us just fine.

We set off in the same embarrassing cavalcade as before, only minus the sun umbrellas, and plus the snorkelling gear. Mr Chester seemingly had no feelings of embarrassment at plonking along the beach in flippers.

The bay was beautiful: a great horseshoe of beach, surrounded by cliffs. Zoë and I hired a couple of sunbeds and an umbrella as far away from the Chesters as we could without being really insulting, then we settled down to sunbathe. We didn't talk much. It was as though the disappointment of last night was still taking time to settle. When we got hot, we swam underwater to the rocks with the snorkels on, and watched bright shoals of fish weave past us, in and out of the sun shadows. It had quite a therapeutic effect on us, somehow.

Lunchtime approached, but the Chesters hadn't brought the picnic hamper this time. They'd got into the idea of lunch at the apartment, followed by a 'siesta', as they now called it. Well, being left alone on the beach suited us fine.

I nudged Zoë as we watched their solid figures head off up the steep path to the road. 'You don't think they're going back to – you know, do you?'

'You know what?'

'Well – back to the flat for a siesta – you know what that usually . . .'

'Oh, *Brianna*! That is just too gross for *words*!' snapped Zoë, as she stalked into the waves for another swim.

There was only one café on the beach: a tiny ramshackle affair, with a sizzling griddle that the owner made the most amazing fried egg and ham sarnies on. As we sat at a table made of crates, swigging Coke and munching, we began to feel a lot better.

'I don't care about last night any more,' announced Zoë.

'Me neither. Put it down to experience.'

'We should have guessed it, though. They were too smooth. They looked like Next adverts. Actually – I didn't really fancy them.'

'Oh yes you *did*!'

'Well – only kind of. Look – let's go back early and get dolled up and go out – *on our own*.'

So that is what we did. And as we swaggered into town that night arm-in-arm we realised something. We no longer felt like newcomers. We no longer felt as though everyone else knew more than we did. We felt like we could take the place on.

'There's nothing quite like surviving smarmy seducers and getting lost and meeting spooky priests to make you feel confident you can handle things,' I said. 'I mean – what else can happen, right?'

We toured the bars. We danced to music from the '60s, we flirted with any bloke who made eye contact, and we had a real laugh. We were chatted up by some lads from Birmingham but decided to escape while it was still at the chat-up stage. We ordered huge ice-creams at a pavement cafe and were asked by no less than three different blokes 'if they could have a lick' (someone should do a survey on the sad lack of male originality). Then we went to another bar, danced to '70s music, and reeled home in the early hours, chewing pitta and lamb we'd brought from a stall, and vowing to do it all again tomorrow.

Dear Pandora ✿ It didn't work
out with the two guys. Don't
ask! What a pair of creeps.
It's great here, though. I'm
really beginning to get into
this lifestyle. Lots of sun
in the day and partying at
night. who needs boys ✿
anyway?!?!* Tons of ✿
        LOve, ✿
     xx Zoë ✿

♥

Alexander The Great

The next morning, obscenely early, Zoë's parents stuck their heads round our bedroom door and announced that two beach days were enough for them; today they wanted to go sight seeing, and they thought we'd like to come, too.

'This island has a formidable history,' began Mr Chester. 'I've been reading all about the Turkish invasion, and it's –'

'*Dad*!' groaned Zoë, head half under her pillow. '*History* is an *exam* subject! History – as far as I'm concerned – is history!'

'Now, Zoë –'

'You and Mum go. Brianna and I need to go to the beach. After we've had some more *sleep*, Dad!'

'Well – if you're sure,' Mr Chester said. 'As long as you stick together, and be careful in the water, and watch the midday sun, and . . .'

Why didn't he just code all his nags? A is for 'stick together', B is for 'don't be late' and so on. Then he could just shout A-F-C-L or whatever at us, and save an awful lot of time.

'And shall we see you back tonight for a Proper Dinner?' Mrs Chester was saying. 'You shouldn't just exist on snacks, you know. I'm doing Shepherd's Pie tonight.'

'Shepherd's . . . ?! Oh, *Mum*. OK. We'll see you tonight.'

The next three days followed the same lovely pattern, with the Chesters leaving before we even woke up. Our tans were getting really impressive, and we told ourselves that the swimming we did was burning off all the ice-creams we were eating. In the scorching heat of midday we'd don our flimsy sarongs and retire into a beach café for shade, ice-cold drinks and lunch, then head back to the shoreline for the afternoon. We were getting on brilliantly together, too. We had such a laugh the whole time.

We went mostly to the beach that was nearest the apartment, partly out of laziness and partly because we'd got to know a few of the people there. We'd done a survey of the beach talent and had several possibilities lined up, but we were in no hurry to take it further than just chatting and flirting and the odd, splashy swim. As the sun went down we'd head back to the apartment to switch off and eat while Zoë's parents wittered on about all the historical sights they'd seen that day. Then we'd have a creative hour or so glamming ourselves up, and hit the island nightlife.

We'd moved on to the Discos now. They had excruciating names like 'Apollo's Wings' and 'Hera's Dive'; they were loud, crude and dated and we loved them. On the fifth night we arranged to meet up with some people from the beach, but it hemmed us in a bit, so the next night we didn't.

We went from dance partner to dance partner – we got bought drinks – we had the odd snog under the star-filled sky and that was enough. I guess Jason and Mark, the beach vampires, had made us wary of getting sucked in by anyone.

I only acted like a real idiot once. I saw Karl, the gorgeous guy from the plane, on the other side of the dance floor. And my stomach did this high-jump up into my throat, and without even saying a word to Zoë and the two lads we were dancing around with, I skirted round the floor towards him, heart pounding. Then when I got to his side I realised it wasn't Karl at all. He just had Karl's loping way of moving, and his hair, and his height. And he also had a ferocious looking girlfriend, who turned and lasered her eyes at me until I'd scuttled away again.

When I got back to Zoë the other two guys had gone but Zoë was very philosophical about it. She just said it was time to move on.

Zoë and I made a brilliant team; we worked together. We'd even worked out a code. We knew what meant 'Clear off – I'm enjoying this' and we understood 'Help – rescue me!'

It was fabulous – the best fun – I could have carried on doing it for ever.

*

We were wandering back to the flat after a riot-
ous, flirtatious Friday night when Zoë announced,
'Tomorrow, Brianna, we take our life in our hands.
We do Beach Sports.'

'Oh, no. Oh, please. Not that horrific banana
thing.' I'd seen tourists being tortured on it. A
speedboat towed a great blown-up banana along at
about 100mph, while the poor mugs who'd actually
paid to get on it got thrown in the water at every
sharp turn.

'Yup,' insisted Zoë. 'I met someone tonight who
told me which beach does the best sports. They
have parascending, and speedboats with rings, and
the banana – the works.'

'Oh, GOODY,' I said, sarcastically. Truth is, I'm
a chronic coward when it comes to anything like
that. Zoë loves all the scary stuff – upside down,
80mph, sheer drops into water – but I'm the original
Theme Park drop-out. Nevertheless, the next morning
saw me on the coastline bus with her, heading for
the Beach-Sports Beach, determined to go through
with it.

'This is on the way to Faliraki, isn't it?' I asked
casually, as we rattled along, holding onto the bus
rails which were already blistering in the heat.

'Yes. The beach is just before you get there. Brianna,
you aren't still on about that lad from the plane,
are you?'

'Might be,' I muttered. 'He was gorgeous.'

'Oh come on Bri, you know what his mates and
he'll be doing now don't you? They'll be holding

♥ 60 ♥

burping competitions and seeing who can pee the furthest.'

'Yeah, I know you're right. It's just you have to admit that Karl was pretty cute.'

'God, Brianna, you're obsessed! Hey – quick – this must be our stop. He said it was by the Vista Hotel.'

We clambered off the bus and headed along the scorching pavement. White tower-block hotels loomed over us. Unlike ancient Lindos, this place had been slapped up in the last few years, with profit in mind. It made a nice change. We peered in all the flashy, tacky restaurants and casinos as we went along, wondering if we'd dare go in any of them.

Then Zoë spotted a signpost: *WATERWORLD*. 'That's it!' she cried triumphantly.

'Original name,' I sneered, as my stomach churned in nervous anticipation.

'Oh, come on, misery. It must be over there – that little landing stage.'

We climbed up some steps and along a rickety boardwalk over the rocks. Basking lizards scattered as we approached; there was no shade anywhere. Emerging onto the landing stage, we looked about us. Two incredibly brown girls were stretched out like cats at one side, silent and unmoving. An equally brown man appeared from a little hut with a palm leaf roof.

'Want a ride, darlin's?' he said, in a Geordie accent.

'Er – yes, please,' said Zoë.

'What's the least scary?' I piped up. 'To start with?'

He grinned at me. 'Got a bad 'ead for heights, 'ave you, luv?'

'No – not for heights. Just for anything too fast.'

'You want to try parascending. It's really – like – restful and nice.' And he pointed across the bay, to where someone was hanging in the vivid blue sky under a little parachute, being towed gently along.

'That looks all right,' I said, relieved. 'Zoë – I'm going first. Before I lose my nerve.'

'OK,' she said, grudgingly. 'Then it's the banana, right?'

The man laughed, and banged on the side of the hut. 'Out here, Alexander, you lazy sod.' And the vision that was Alexander materialised in the doorway of the hut. Tall, browner even than the sleeping girls, with short, curly black hair, and wearing not much more than a thong. I could sense Zoë's jaw practically hit the deck beside me. He had the kind of romantic look that Zoë loves. I'm not that keen on it, myself. His nose could have been a girl's.

'So,' he said, picking up a couple of life jackets, 'parascending, yes? You girls want to fly?'

He helped us into the jackets. He took a very long time buckling up Zoë's. Meanwhile, I'd paid the fee and stepped into a waiting motorboat; the Geordie was already in the driver's seat, fiddling with the controls. Then Alexander stepped into the boat and made a great show of gallantly handing Zoë into her seat.

The boat started up, moving out into the bay. Oh, Lord, I thought. No going back now.

'So,' said Alexander, showing all his white teeth, 'you're English, yes?'

'Yes,' simpered Zoë. 'What about you?'

'My mother was Greek, my father Australian,' he announced solemnly, as though this was the most stunning genetic combination in the Western World. And you had to admit, it was a pretty winning mixture. His mum must have passed on the melting dark eyes and smouldering expression, while his dad let him have the height and broad shoulders. Some parents can be OK.

'That's . . . amazing,' Zoë breathed.

I stared over at her, concerned. She didn't usually talk in that breathy-husky voice. One look at her face told me the truth – she was gone – hooked. This was far worse than the beach vampires, this was for real. But I didn't have time to worry about it, because the Geordie had slowed the boat right down and was saying, 'Right then. Lift-off.'

Alexander wrestled me into this little seat with a harness, and then pushed me gently towards the back of the boat. 'Now,' he said, 'the boat speeds up a little – and you just step backwards, yes?'

'Step off the boat?' I squeaked. 'You're joking!'

'No. I don't joke. You step off and then you – float. It will be fine.' He smiled meltingly at me. 'Trust me.'

I wouldn't trust *you* further than I could *throw* you, I thought grimly, as the boat started to gain speed.

'Go on,' he repeated. 'One little step back.'

So I shut my eyes, and stepped, and to my amazement, my feet stayed perfectly dry. I just floated out behind the boat, climbing higher and higher. Gradually, the boat gained speed, and as it did Alexander let the rope out, and I went higher still. Then I just hung there, swaying slightly, looking at the amazing scene below, all the tiny people and the bright, dolls' umbrellas, and the little boat, attached to me by its long line. It was fabulous. I'm not brilliant at heights, but this was different. I felt exhilarated, uplifted.

After the boat had circled the bay once, with me floating behind, it began to slow down, and I could see Alexander reeling me in. That was a short trip, I thought, disappointed. Lower and lower I drifted, until I came right down to the level of the boat and my feet splashed into the sea. 'Oh, God, I'm going *under*,' I wailed, as I ploughed deeper into the waves, then suddenly the boat shot forward again and I rose out of the water and up into the air, like a seabird taking flight. It was thrilling.

After another tour of the bay, they reeled me in for good. 'That was *unbelievable*!' I jabbered to Zoë, as I struggled out of the harness. 'When you're up there, the view is just stunning, and the breeze . . .'

She hadn't heard a word I was saying. Her eyes were fixed on Alexander's face as he took the harness off me and turned towards her. It took him about five months to fit her into it, doing all the buckles up in slow motion, then triple-checking them. 'Now move to the back, like your friend did,' he said. 'I'm with you.' And he was, too. You couldn't have slid a sheet of paper between them.

'OK, step back. Be brave,' he whispered to her. 'Be as brave as you are beautiful.'

I was hoping Zoë would come to her senses and burst out laughing when she heard this, but no; she gazed at him as if she might learn the secret of existence from his eyes, then she stepped back, off the boat, and floated off into the blue. He waved at her in slow motion as she rose higher; every wave was packed with emotion. You didn't wave me off, did you, I thought grumpily. He turned to me. 'Your friend,' he said simply, 'is exquisite.' Then he sat at the end of the boat and watched her, as if anything else would hurt his eyes.

♥

Caught Between Friendship
And Lust

I could hardly bear to witness the reeling in and unbuckling procedure. It was like Zoë was an incredibly precious gift being unwrapped. Alexander kept congratulating her, as though she'd pulled off something unique. Then they sat together in the prow, murmuring together, so the only space left for me was in the front next to the Geordie, whose one topic of conversation was the havoc that barnacles wreaked on his boat bottom. We chugged slowly back to shore, and came to a stop alongside the landing stage. It had suddenly filled up; there were about six boys crowded onto it, jostling each other and messing about. The two cat-girls had rolled right to the edge of the wooden platform in fastidious disgust.

'I *told* you it was them,' came a loud, cocky voice. 'Hi girls! It's us!'

And I realised to my delight that the crowd of lads was none other than Reg and friends from the airport. Eagerly, I craned my neck to look for Karl. He was at the back looking even more lush with a tan and shorts. Suddenly, I felt incredibly excited.

I clambered up onto the landing stage, making it

more crowded still. Alexander half-lifted Zoë up from the boat, and very slowly set her down.

'Been up, have you?' demanded Reg. 'Parascending? What d'you reckon to it?'

'Great,' I said. 'Lovely.'

'How's the holiday been so far, then?' he asked, moving in closer and grinning right at me. His sudden friendliness took me slightly aback. I guess he felt sharing a plane gave us a real link.

'Er – OK. Great. Terrific.' I moved sideways, a bit further from him, and a bit nearer to Karl.

He followed me. 'Your tan looks good. Hey – they browner than us, lads? What d'you reckon?' He got hold of my arm, and compared it to his. He seemed strangely reluctant to let go.

'I reckon the girls look better,' said a tall blond boy, stepping forward and standing practically nose to nose with Zoë. 'A lot better. You look kind of roasted, Reg mate.'

'Yeah, well, at least I go brown,' Reg retorted. 'You blond-boys don't tan at all.'

'We were just going out on the banana,' said the blond guy, talking straight at Zoë. 'Have you tried it yet? It's wicked.'

'No,' said Zoë, distractedly. She was watching Alexander help secure the boat.

'Why don't we all go out? It takes eight. If we leave Reg behind, there'd be room for the rest of us.'

'No-one's leaving me behind, Mike, you prat,' roared Reg, shoving him good-naturedly into Zoë.

Zoë stepped back, and gave Mike her best glacial-maiden stare. 'Do you *mind*?' she spat.

'Not in the slightest,' said Mike. 'Come on, let's go for a whirl on the banana.'

'No thank you,' she said, icily.

'I thought you wanted to go out on the banana?' I put in. Dammit, this was my chance to legitimately squeeze up close to Karl, and she was just chucking it away!

She turned to glare at me. 'I've just changed my mind.'

'Oh, change it back again, go on,' said Mike. 'Your friend wants to go.'

'Yeah, let's do it,' said Karl, looking straight at me.

'Have you tried it yet?' I asked him, looking straight back.

'Yeah – once,' he answered, smiling. 'I came off twice.'

'Let's go, shall we?' broke in Reg, beckoning to the Geordie.

'Count me out,' said Zoë, in a super-snotty voice.

'Oh, go on,' said Mike. 'I'll make sure you don't drown.'

Reg jeered, and gave Mike another shove, so that he collided into Zoë once more. Zoë staggered backwards, swore violently, teetered for one heart-stopping moment on the extreme edge of the landing stage, then fell into the water with a huge splash.

There was a horrified pause. Then we turned as one to see Alexander executing a perfect dive off the side of his boat. Seconds later, he broke the surface of the water, clutching Zoë in a full-blown life-saver's hold. Three pairs of hands reached over the side to haul Zoë to safety. She lay gasping like a mermaid on the wooden planks of the landing stage. Alexander clambered out of the water, pushed me out of the way, and threw himself down beside her. 'Are you all right?' he breathed into her ear.

Zoë turned to him, weakly. 'Yes,' she whispered. 'Thank you.'

Alexander sprang to his feet, all wet and heroic-looking. '*WHICH ONE OF YOU ANIMALS THREW HER IN??*' he roared.

'Nobody threw her in, mate, she fell,' said Reg.

'*SOMEBODY PUSHED HER!*'

'Oh, for God's sake. It was an accident.'

Meanwhile, Zoë had staggered to her feet. 'You *idiots*,' she wailed. 'I could have hit my head on the side, I could've . . .'

'Oh, come on,' broke in Mike. 'I mean – I'm really sorry that it happened, but . . .'

'I grazed my *knee*!' screeched Zoë. 'You gits, you pathetic . . . God, it's just so typical . . .'

Alexander put a protective arm round her, murmuring, 'It's OK, it's OK.'

'Look, it was my fault,' admitted Reg, diplomatically. 'But there's not exactly a lot of room on this platform to mess around on . . .'

'No, there isn't,' said Alexander, fiercely. 'And now you can go and mess around somewhere else. You're banned. Go on, get out.'

'*Banned?* What the hell for?'

'We were just having a laugh and . . .'

'You saw it,' said Karl, turning to me. 'Can't you tell him it wasn't deliberate?'

Oh, great. Caught between friendship and lust. Zoë stopped coughing out seawater to glare at me. Friendship – I supposed – had to win.

'Look, they were stupid,' I said to Alexander, 'but there's no need to . . .'

'They were stupid. That's all I need to know,' interrupted Alexander grandly, tightening his protective arm round Zoë. 'Go on, get out, and don't come back.'

The boys knew there was no point in arguing. Alexander probably had a panic button in his hut with a direct link to the local police heavies. It was quite pitiful, watching them all swear bad-temperedly and troop off the landing stage, deprived of their trips on the banana for the rest of the holiday. It was especially pitiful seeing Karl disappear. In fact, I could have cried.

It would have been pretty crass to get angry with Zoë, all dripping wet and shaken as she was. But it was hard to feel nice about her, either. Alexander and she carried on whispering together for a bit, then he came over to me, and told me to get her back to the apartment safely. 'She's very shaken up,' he said, tenderly. 'You be good to her.'

So I carried our beach-bag all the way to the bus-stop and not very graciously gave Zoë the one empty seat when the bus finally arrived. As the bus pulled away, she appeared to make a total recovery.

'Did Alexander say anything about me when I was up in the air?' she asked urgently.

'Yeah,' I replied, sulkily. 'He said you were a real sucker to get taken in by all the corn he was spieling out.'

Zoë pinched my arm viciously. '*Brianna! Tell* me.'

'*OUCH*! Gerroff. He said you were exquisite. Then he went off into a kind of trance. Maybe he's a Buddhist or something . . .' But Zoë had gone off into her own kind of trance, and stopped hearing me. We bumped along for a bit, and then the unfairness of the whole situation got hold of me again.

'You didn't have to be so fierce with those guys,' I said, loudly. 'You knew I really liked Karl.'

'Oh, for *heaven's sake*, Brianna,' she snapped. 'He's an idiot. They're all idiots.'

'Maybe,' I replied. 'You didn't give me a chance to find out, did you?'

'Find out? What more proof d'you need? I could have *drowned* if Alexander hadn't rescued me.' And she glowed at the memory.

'It wasn't Karl who pushed you off,' I muttered, then I gave up, and stared out of the grimy bus window at the cacti and the goats.

♥

Give Me A Break

Zoë and I arrived back at the apartment in almost total silence. In fact there was a distinct rift between us. Though I'm not sure Zoë cared – or even knew – about it, she was off in fantasy land, thinking about Alexander.

Mr and Mrs Chester were already there. Mrs Chester was seated at the terrace table doing something painstaking with a pile of red peppers, and Mr Chester was polishing his sandals. Seriously, he was.

'Oh, good,' beamed Mrs Chester as we wandered in. 'In good time for dinner! Look – I've gone all Mediterranean!'

Well, wow, I thought grumpily. Shepherd's pie with peppers in it.

'Had a nice day, girls?' asked Mr Chester.

'Great thanks,' said Zoë, absently. 'Er – Mum? What time's dinner? Only I'm going out at eight . . .'

I'm going out. Oh, terrific. And no prizes for guessing who with.

'Oh, seven-ish, dear. You've got plenty of time.'

But Zoë looked panic stricken. 'I'd better get ready first then,' she cried, and made a rush for the bathroom.

She was in there for hours. As I sat on the terrace wall waiting bad-temperedly, I swear I could feel the salt drying on my skin and my tan flaking off. When she finally came out, she barely glanced at me as she rushed by, let alone apologised for using up all the hot water. Which, when I went for my shower, I discovered she had done.

And I *hate* washing my hair in cold water. It never rinses properly. I stomped back to our bedroom, grumpier still. Zoë stood there transfixed in front of the mirror, blow-drying her hair as though her life depended on it.

'So,' I began, 'you're meeting your Greek god tonight, are you?'

She turned to me, pleadingly. 'Oh, Brianna, you don't mind, do you? He said he'd pick me up at eight. On his bike.'

'And will Daddy swallow that?' I said a bit nastily. 'He'll come out with his "you girls stick together" routine, won't he?'

Her face fell. 'Oh, God, I hadn't thought of that. What shall I do?'

'Drag Alexander up to meet them, I suppose,' I said, softening. 'He's such a charmer, he'll win them round. Then maybe you could just walk into Lindos, if they're worried about the bike.' Boy, was I magnanimous and helpful or what?

Zoë rushed over and hugged me. 'Oh, Brianna, you're *great*! Thank you. And maybe you can say we spent the day together, all three of us, and how nice he is . . .'

Don't push your luck, I thought sourly.

'And look – can I borrow your red dress tonight?'

Dinner was not brilliant. Mrs Chester's Mediterranean effort was pretty dried up and unappetising. Zoë hardly ate or spoke. Her eyes were fixed on some distant plain, far away from us. Mr and Mrs Chester just about wrung it out of her that she was going out tonight with someone called Alexander who ran a beach sports centre. Then they turned their attention to me, in a really irritating, consoling sort of way.

'Oh, well, Brianna,' said Mr Chester kindly. 'Never mind. I'm sure you could do with an early night. You girls have been burning the candle at both ends, you have.'

'And we're staying in too,' added Mrs Chester, 'so you'll have company.'

Oh, terrific.

'We had a grand game of Scrabble last night. Do you like Scrabble, Brianna?'

Oh, *terrific*.

I glared at Zoë as she sailed past me to the bedroom to do a last minute make-up check, but she didn't notice. As I was clearing the table, I heard a discreet little 'parp' from the road outside, and then I heard someone running up the steps, and a light tap on the door.

Loverboy had arrived.

I opened the door to him. He'd brought flowers. For Mrs Chester. What a total *creep*.

♥ 74 ♥

He was wearing a white shirt unbuttoned practically to the naval, which made him look even browner, and these baggy, Turkish looking trousers, like a dancer. And he oozed charm and sincerity. The Chesters were completely taken in by him. Mrs Chester cooed over the flowers and wheeled out the sparkling wine and cashew nuts once again. Mr Chester seemed fascinated by the fact that Alexander was half Greek – he kept asking him about his mother, and how long he'd lived on the island.

After ten ultra-charming minutes, during which I had difficulty keeping my dinner down, Alexander steered Zoë towards the door, promising to 'show her my beautiful island' and look after her.

'You look fabulous,' he murmured, as they escaped. 'My lady in red.'

'Oh, *please*,' I thought, in total revulsion. 'Ditch him *now*, Zoë – he'll start singing it in a minute!' But Zoë merely smiled moonily, and shut the door behind them. And then I heard, 'Shall I get the Scrabble board out?'

I had an extremely early night that night, which was just as well, because Zoë woke me up at 2am by landing on my bed.

'Brianna? Are you asleep?'

'Not any more,' I grumbled. 'Well – how was it?'

'He is *astounding*,' she announced, solemnly. 'He is just the most romantic, fabulous, gorgeous bloke I have ever met in my whole life.'

'So it wasn't too bad then?'

'We danced under the moon,' she chanted. 'We drank wine under the stars. He is just so *beautiful* to look at, and he's kind, and thoughtful – he bought me this flower.' And she thrust a rose into my face. *More* flowers, I thought sourly. Must have shares in a flower shop.

'We went to this tiny little bar and just talked for *hours*. I've never been able to be that open with a bloke before, never. It was like we'd known each other for years. Then this guitarist started up and we danced on this tiny dance floor, just the two of us, and Alexander kept asking him to play these wonderful, sad songs . . . Then we walked along the beach. It was so beautiful. He said if he ever had to live away from the sea, he thought he'd die. He loves the sea. He says he's only really complete by the sea. He had such a sad childhood.'

He would have, I thought, sourer still.

'He told me all about it. His father left when he was tiny. He told me it made it hard for him to trust people – to – to love anyone, to give himself to anyone. But he felt – he said – he thought it might be different with me.'

Oh, *spare us*. 'Zoë,' I snapped, 'didn't it occur to you that this was all a bit *deep* for a first date?'

She looked at me as though I'd punched her. 'What do you mean?'

'I mean going on about his sad past and how it might be different with you. I mean – isn't it all a bit *sudden*?'

Zoë studied my face, full of pity. 'You're such a cynic, Brianna. Don't you believe that two people can just know from the start that they're right for each other? Don't you believe in love at first sight?'

'Oh, for heaven's sake, Zoë. Yes, maybe. But you were the one going on about not taking holiday romances seriously, and now you're . . .'

Zoë got to her feet, frostily. 'I'm going outside,' she said. 'To look at the stars.'

Dear Pandora 🐷 I think I'm in L♡VE ! I have met the most amazing boy. Half Greek, half Australian. He is completely gorgeous, and he treats me as though I'm a princess. I feel fabulous when I'm with him it's unreal. Brianna is being a real cow about it. I suppose she's jealous, but I didn't expect her to be this mean. Wish you were here. Loads of LOVE Zoë ♡♡♡♡♡♡♡ xxx Zoë

♥

Gooseberry Fool

I woke up the next morning determined to be more tolerant, and Zoë had obviously decided to be nice to me too, so we had a reasonable time getting breakfast together.

'When are you seeing Alexander again?' I made myself ask, as we spooned Greek cornflakes into our mouths.

'Well,' said Zoë, going all ingratiating, 'he'd like me – US – to go to WATERWORLD again today, and be – be with him while he works.'

'Oh, great. So I sit there like a big gooseberry, do I?'

'Oh, come on, Bri. It's a nice beach. You and I will be able to swim together and stuff, and he said he'd give us free rides and so on. I mean, he'll be *working*. It's not as though I'll be hanging round him the whole time.'

What's that irritating old saying? 'Famous last words'? As soon as we drew close to WATERWORLD, Zoë got that glazed, brain-dead expression she'd had last night, and fixed her eyes on the distant figure of Alexander as though no one else existed. Hanging round him? She looked like she wanted to achieve osmosis with him.

As soon as he spotted her he rushed over, grabbed her, and swung her right off her feet and into the air in greeting. Not a guy to do things by halves, obviously. Zoë was giggling delightedly, gazing down at him, while he looked up at her with an expression full of joy and passion. Then he set her back on her feet, treated her to one more super-smouldering expression, and they were off on this huge, saliva-swapping, five-hour snog. The Geordie practically had to prise them apart to get Alexander to start marshalling the queue of tourists that had formed on the deck.

'Stay here, angel,' Alexander whispered to Zoë, as he clambered into the boat. 'I won't be long.' Then he flashed his teeth at her, and disappeared over the side.

Zoë wrapped her arms round herself and gave a little whimper of joy, then wandered over to the edge of the landing stage. The bronzed cat-girls had disappeared. Zoë stretched out in their place. 'Come on, Bri,' she called. 'Let's do some sunbathing.'

I flumped down beside her. Try to be generous, I lectured myself. Just because you *are* totally and utterly left out doesn't mean you have to be all immature and *act* it.

I got out my suncream. 'Want me to oil your back?' I asked.

'Mmm,' she said.

'Which protection level d'you want?' We'd been dead scientific about staggering the protection levels. 'Eight or twelve?'

'Mmmm.'

I gave up. The thing is, Zoë wasn't really bothered if I was generous or not. She wasn't bothered if I talked to her or not. To be honest, she wouldn't have turned a hair if an alien spaceship had suddenly beamed me up on board. She'd wanted to get me along today because she'd have felt guilty about abandoning me, but that was the only reason. All she cared about now was waiting for Alexander. I slapped on some suncream, slipped off my straps and flopped down on my front to get my back brown. The landing stage was very hard and very uncomfortable to lie on.

By my side, Zoë lay propped up on one elbow, her eyes glued to the little speedboat as it shot around the bay. Soon, the boat got bigger, closer, then it roared up to the platform and stopped. Alexander sprang onto the landing stage, stretched out alongside an ecstatic Zoë and wrapped himself round her, and they were off on another marathon snogging session.

I'm not at all sure how much more of this I can take, I thought bitterly, trying to block my ears to all the dodgy necking sounds right next to me. I'd feel a lot less alone if I was *on* my own.

Soon, the Geordie was yelling about getting the next boatload organised, and Alexander very slowly disentangled himself from Zoë and stood up.

'There's room for you in the boat this time!' he beamed, doing a quick head count of punters. 'Coming for a spin?'

'Come on, Brianna,' said Zoë. 'You come too.'

It was all getting worse and worse. I had to go along

or I'd look like a real sour grapes merchant, but it meant sitting in the back next to two ten-year-old boys, while the two lovers practically ate each other in front of me.

'We're going parascending,' announced one of the little boys solemnly.

'Great,' I muttered.

'Are you?'

'No, not this time.'

'Why are you in the boat then?'

I fixed them with a wild stare. 'I really don't know,' I said.

'Look at those two!' said one of the boys, shocked, as Alexander and Zoë got even more entwined.

The other little boy was staring at me unblinkingly. 'Why haven't you got a boyfriend?' he asked.

I gazed hopelessly out to sea, and thought about diving over the edge and not coming up again. Come on, I muttered to myself, don't let things get out of perspective. It's worked out for Zoë, but not for you this time, that's all. No big deal.

Then the Geordie slowed the boat right down, and dug Alexander in the side. He did this casually, without even looking at him, almost as if it was a routine – as if he was used to his business partner being wrapped round a girl. I stared at Alexander as he buckled the first little boy into his harness. I bet you pick up someone new every week, I thought angrily. The reason you've got such an incredibly smooth, polished technique is because you practise it so often.

Alexander supervised the little boy's ascent into the sky, then went straight back to mauling Zoë. He was all over her like olive oil, and not the extra-virgin variety, either.

The boat roared along, and I glared at the back of Alexander's head as his mouth made contact with Zoë's. You oily git, I thought savagely.

After the two little boys had had their trip, we all returned to shore. This time there was a whole crowd waiting to go parascending, so Zoë and I had to sit on the landing stage again.

'Let's go and get a drink,' I suggested. 'Some of those beach cafés look good.'

'Oh, but the boat'll be back in a few minutes. And I promised Alexander I'd be here.'

'Zoë,' I exploded. 'Are you planning to be here *every* time his damn boat draws up at the side?'

She smiled endearingly at me. 'Can't you go and get some drinks and bring them back here?'

That did it. She was so obsessed it was sickening. I got to my feet and walked away without a word. I stomped across the blistering sand to the nearest café and ordered the most expensive fruit cocktail drink I could see on the menu. It had so many paper umbrellas and bits of pineapple sticking out of the top I could barely get my mouth round it, but it didn't make me feel better.

OK, I thought. This can't go on. Time to take stock and work things out. And I made up a sort of agenda in my head, chewing thoughtfully on bits of mango between each point.

Point 1. Through no fault of your own the holiday, which you were enjoying so enormously, has suddenly gone seriously downhill. Now you have to work out how to salvage it

Point 2. Whatever you think about the creep, Zoë's gone on him. She wants to spend every waking moment with him, and probably some sleeping ones too.

Point 3. You can't stop that. If you try she'll hate you for it.

Point 4. She is TRYING not to leave you out. She's asked you to come along with her today. But tagging along makes you feel about as exciting as an old sock.

Point 5. You have no alternative. You have to leave them alone together, partly for their sakes, but mainly for YOURS.

Then I got wearily to my feet, and returned to the landing stage. I even bought Zoë an ice-cold can of Coke on the way back. Let no one say that I was being childish and vindictive about all this.

'Zoë,' I announced, as I sat down beside her and handed her the drink, 'I think I'm going to head back now. I really do feel three's a crowd right now.'

Zoë looked at me guiltily over the Coke can rim. 'Oh, Bri, are you sure? Alexander said he'd let us have a go on the banana, the first time there were some spaces free.'

'Oh – you want to go on the banana now, do you? You didn't fancy it yesterday.'

'Oh, Bri, come *on* – I'd just nearly been brained on the rocks when I said that . . .'

'OK, OK, forget it, I didn't mean it. No, I'm going to get the bus back. I don't really like this beach. I'll find some lunch at the apartment, and then go down to our beach for the rest of the day.'

Zoë tried unsuccessfully to repress the relief that played across her face. 'OK, then,' she said. 'You'll probably meet up with some people we know there, won't you?'

'Probably,' I said, stiffly. 'Anyway – see you.' And I left. When I'd got onto the boardwalk I turned back meaning to wave, but Alexander's boat had got in and the two were welded together in yet another all-out embrace. So I didn't bother.

♥

Son Et Lumière

I was incredibly relieved to find the apartment empty when I finally got back, and I headed straight for the shower – a cold one. The island buses must be at their most uncomfortable in the middle of the day. I'd felt like a clay pot being fired in a kiln.

Then I grabbed a ragbag lunch and went and lay down on my cool bed to eat it. As I chewed on bits of cheese and fruit, I thought about how much fun it had been the last few days, just Zoë and I slamming around together, and then I thought about her with Alexander, and the very final way Karl had walked off the landing stage at *WATERWORLD*, and tears of chronic self-pity started to trickle down my nose.

'It's 'cos you don't have to put up a front any more,' I told myself dolefully. 'You're not that unhappy, just letting it out.' But the tears seemed to go on for quite a while, and then I found myself drifting into sleep. It was quite a relief, somehow.

I was woken by a cup of tea being rattled about two centimetres from my ear. 'Having a little siesta, are you?' beamed Mr Chester. 'And why not. This weather is absolutely punishing, if you ask me. Here's a cuppa for you.'

'Oh, thank you, that's lovely,' I said, struggling to a sitting position and hoping my eyes weren't too red.

'Where's Zoë?' asked Mr Chester, trying to seem unconcerned.

'Oh, she's still at the beach sports place – with Alexander.'

'Ah,' he replied, in a voice full of understanding and pity. 'They seem to have hit it off, don't they?'

'Yes,' I said weakly, taking a sip of my tea.

'Well look, Brianna, it's nearly four o'clock . . .' I gaped at him. I'd been asleep for over two hours! 'Mother and I are going to drive into Rhodes and see the *Son et Lumière* there. Did you know we'd hired a little car?'

I shook my head, feebly.

'It makes sightseeing so much more convenient. So why don't you put your togs on, and come with us?'

'Oh, but it's – that's very kind of you but I thought I'd go down to the local beach and . . .'

'But the sun'll be going down in a few hours. And you don't want to be heading off there on your own.'

Mrs Chester had appeared in the doorway. 'Not on your own, dear,' she echoed.

Being ON YOUR OWN was one of the Chesters' great taboos. They had this pathetic, parental belief that nothing could happen to a girl as long as she had a friend beside her. They didn't realise you usually got up to a lot more if you had a mate egging you on, and I suppose it wasn't in our interests to enlighten them.

'Come on,' said Mr Chester encouragingly. 'We

thought we'd treat ourselves to a spot of dinner first. There's some quite nice restaurants in the old part of Rhodes Town.'

What chance did I stand? They were being so kind it would have been churlish in the extreme to refuse. So five o'clock saw me 'with my togs on', waiting on the terrace as Mrs Chester wrote a note for Zoë. 'Goodness knows what time she'll be back,' she said, smiling at me indulgently, 'the naughty girl!'

I smiled back wanly. Then we headed down to the car-park and Mr Chester unlocked the hired car. We got in and sat in its broiling heat as he unwound a selection of tea-towels from the steering wheel. 'It gets too hot to hold in the heat of the day unless you take a few precautionary measures,' he explained, as he handed the tea-towels one by one to Mrs Chester, who folded them neatly.

Precautionary measures, I thought gloomily. They'll carve that on his gravestone.

Mr Chester drove at about five miles an hour, slowing down to even less than that whenever any other vehicle appeared on the same road as him. Most of the conversation on the way to Rhodes Town was take up with how hard it was to drive on the 'wrong' side, and how clever Mr Chester was to do it at all. At every junction, every turning, Mrs Chester would pat his hand and say, 'Remember to keep to the right, dear!' and laugh, and he'd laugh back and say, 'I will, dear, I will!'

I was ready to commit suicide by the time we got to the town and parked, I can tell you.

But when we walked into Old Rhodes, I was quite pleasantly surprised. It was far more lively than I expected it to be. There were crowds of people milling about, going in and out of restaurants and bars, and loads of interesting looking little shops, all spilling out onto the pavement and all open till late.

After a while, though, all the bustle and life just made me more depressed. If I could have been there with Zoë, or some gorgeous guy – someone like Karl – it would have been the most amazing fun. But I was there with the Chesters, and that was a bit like looking out from behind bars at everyone else's fun.

After a lot of walking about, expressing a lot of disapproval at all the anarchic little shops ('The thing is,' said Mrs Chester, 'with somewhere like Marks and Spencer, you know exactly where you are') they selected the most staid looking restaurant they could find. Mr Chester only changed his mind about where we should sit once, quite a record for him. Then he made me cringe by cross-examining the waiter on just about every item on the menu, and then ordering plain steak.

As the waiter cleared our plates, Mr Chester whispered something to him. I didn't think much of it – I was too busy jealously watching a besotted couple opposite. But then five minutes later the waiter came back and plonked before me a massive Knickerbocker Glory, complete with three flaring sparklers. Everyone – absolutely everyone – in the restaurant turned to admire it and stare at me, while Mrs Chester squealed and clapped her hands. Mr Chester raised his camera and called out, 'Let's have a smile, Brianna, while your face is so nicely lit up!'

I sat there baring my teeth, muttering 'thank you – it's lovely', and wanting to *die*. Everyone'll think it's my birthday, I thought, choked. I look like the sort of deeply sad person who spends her birthday on her own with two *parents*. Someone else's *parents*.

When the sparklers had finally fizzled out, I gagged down some synthetic cream and nutty goo, then said I really couldn't manage any more. Luckily, no one wanted coffee. Mr Chester paid the bill and I shot out of the restaurant, escaping thankfully into the anonymous darkness.

The *Son et Lumière* was being staged at an old castle near the city walls. Mr Chester laboriously explained to me that 'son et lumière' meant sound and light, and it was about the final Turkish invasion of Rhodes. Wow, I thought, big thrills. I was yawning before it even started, and when it did get going – well, sleep would have been a rave in comparison. The 'son' was a load of naff, warlike sound effects. And the 'lumière' was someone flicking lights on and off in different parts of the castle. For two hours.

Mr and Mrs Chester sat engrossed. At the height of the battle, a spotlight made a wall gradually turn red, and Mrs Chester nudged me, saying, 'I think that's meant to be the flow of blood.'

Just as well she put me right. There was me thinking it was supposed to be ketchup.

The only good thing about the whole event was a tribe of stray cats, who put on their own show at the same time, chasing each other in and out of the bushes. When the thing was finally over I went up to stroke one of the kittens, but Mrs Chester called out, 'Don't touch it, dear. These island cats are full of diseases.'

When we got back to the car, I thanked them as warmly as I could for the evening. They really had been very kind to me, and done everything they could think of to cheer me up. The fact that it had left me feeling twice as bad as before was absolutely not their fault.

There was no sign that Zoë had returned to the apartment. Mrs Chester's note was still there on the table, propped against a stone jar. It wasn't until I went into our room that I realised she had been back, and in a tearing hurry. Towels and her bikini were strewn across the floor, makeup lay scattered, topless, across the windowsill.

And when I opened the wardobe, I saw that my white dress was missing.

♥

No Escape

I was woken up this time just before dawn by Zoë hissing into my ear, 'You're wrong about Alexander, Brianna. You're so wrong.'

I groaned and rolled over.

'I know you think he's coming on too strong too soon. But he is the most sensitive, caring guy I've ever met, and – look, Brianna – wake up! I have to talk to you.'

I groaned again, and rolled back to face her. 'What about?' I muttered.

'Look – I feel really bad about you being left on your own today—'

'I wasn't on my own. I was with your mum and dad.'

'Oh, God – well, that's worse then. But something's happened, Brianna – I mean, this is special – it's like nothing I've ever felt before.'

'OK, OK.'

'If you felt like I felt about someone – I'd be happy for you. I mean – I know it means you get left on your own and everything – but it's so *special* – and I can't . . .'

I rolled away again. 'It's OK, Zoë,' I muttered. 'Let me sleep.'

The whole Chester family were having breakfast on the terrace when I crawled out of bed later. From the way Zoë smiled innocently at me I had this strong feeling that she'd been engaged in some kind of damage limitation exercise with her parents. They'd been ticking her off for abandoning me, she'd been giving them *her* side, and they'd bought it.

'So,' said Mr Chester breezily as I sat down. 'What's on the agenda for today?'

'Well,' said Zoë, just as though she *hadn't* been telling him all about it three minutes earlier, 'Alexander's asked us both out on a big boat. He's doing a sort of excursion thing today round all the islands.'

'And he'll let you girls go, will he?' chipped in Mrs Chester. 'That's nice.'

Yes, but it's not 'you girls' is it? I thought savagely. It's Zoë – and her tagalong friend with no one to talk to.

'Or,' said Mr Chester firmly, watching my face, 'mother and I thought we'd drive back to Rhodes Town. It's the last day we've got the car for. I'd like to walk round the fortification walls on the outskirts of the city.'

Oh, *groovy*.

Everyone looked at me expectantly. I was obviously supposed to select one of these mouthwatering options. And all I really wanted to do was be left on my own.

'Well,' I began, 'if it's OK I might just go down to the beach for a swim and . . .'

'Oh, you can't stay here, dear,' said Mrs Chester firmly. 'Not *on your own*.'

Great. So Zoë's safe with that oversexed git but I'm in grave danger if I'm *on my own*. That's just great. But I knew when I was beaten. Their taboo about being solo was insurmountable. So I went for the Rhodes option. Anything was better than sitting at the back of a boat like some kind of sad voyeur as Zoë and Alexander got as close as they could without actually merging.

Zoë danced off to *WATERWORLD*, with lots of virtuous little 'Are you *sure* you won't come, Brianna?'s, and Mr and Mrs Chester and I walked to the car together.

On the way, I noticed a distinct briskening of attitude towards me. They obviously felt that I wasn't being left out – I was *choosing* to be left out. In their view, Zoë and Alexander had asked me on a nice trip, and I'd opted not to go. In their minds, Zoë and Alexander were still at the holding-hands stage, with the odd stolen kiss. Nor was there any way they'd learn the truth, either. After all, having her parents around wouldn't so much cramp Zoë's making-out style as crush it into total oblivion.

After the usual snail's pace journey, we arrived in Rhodes Town, parked, and set off along the barren route between the fortification walls. They were huge, towering, endless. It was like trekking along some great, hot gutter.

'What an amazing military conception,' enthused Mr Chester, gazing around him. 'You see how it works? The enemy breach the outer wall and make it into the middle, here. Then the knights inside—' he pointed at the city wall '—have them TRAPPED.'

We passed a large pile of stone cannonballs. 'That's how they'd polish them off,' he went on. 'Cannon and burning pitch – brilliant, brilliant.'

Mrs Chester looked up at the walls nervously. 'It must have been fearful,' she piped.

'Absolutely,' he agreed, happily. 'And if the cannons didn't finish you off, the knights' swords would. Just imagine being trapped down here while HOARDS of the enemy swept down on you from above. Hundreds of men must have been butchered on this very spot. THOUSANDS!'

I was beginning to feel really claustrophobic and spooked. I thought about all the blood soaking into the ground we were walking on. I could almost hear the screams, ricochetting off the walls.

'Why don't we crack open the flask of tea now?' beamed Mr Chester. 'I could do with whetting my whistle.' He perched on a cannonball in the shade of a stunted tree, and Mrs Chester sat beside him.

'Come on, Brianna love,' she said, patting the cannonball next to her. 'D'you fancy a sandwich?'

They took fifteen minutes having their grisly picnic. Mr Chester read out details of some of the worst massacres from a little guide book as we ate. Then he stood up, and said, 'Come on ladies! Nearly half way!'

HALF WAY?! I couldn't believe we had to walk as far again.

We plodded on as the sadistic sun glared down on us, and the terrain got worse. Builders had been shoring up places where the walls had started to collapse, and their rubble was everywhere. As we clambered over a pile of planks and broken bricks, Mrs Chester asked, 'Are you sure we're meant to be here, dear?'

'Yes, of course we're meant to be here,' Mr Chester snapped. 'There are little signposts along the way.'

'But they stopped some time ago, dear,' ventured Mrs Chester. 'I noticed.'

Mr Chester harumphed and stalked on. Then we rounded a corner and faced a sheer drop into some sort of excavation site.

'Ah,' he admitted. 'Right. We'd better turn back.'

Mrs Chester looked panic stricken. 'What – *all* the way back?'

'Well, there's no other way out is there?' he snapped.

'But it's getting on for *midday*!' she wailed. 'You know I can't stand the midday sun!' Midday sun for Mrs Chester held the same fears as daybreak did for Dracula. She couldn't be out in it. She reckoned it would finish her off.

Mr Chester looked frantically about him. His role as protector was under threat. 'Look!' he suddenly exclaimed. 'The ground's much higher over the outer wall – look at those people!'

People were sailing along on the other side of the wall, visible from the waist up. Some of them looked down at us curiously.

'If we can just shin up that wall,' said Mr Chester, eagerly, 'we'll barely have a drop to the other side.'

'Shin up . . . ? Drop . . . ?' faltered Mrs Chester. 'Oh, Derek, I *can't*.'

'Yes you can, Marjorie,' said Mr Chester, looking over her head at me with a this-is-an-emergency-situation-help-me-out expression. 'Look at the rubble piled there – nearly to the top of the wall. No problem. Now, I'll climb over first, and then Brianna can help heave you up from below.'

Oh, great. Oh, terrific. Brianna can help heave you up from below. The three of us staggered up the rubble, and then with much straining and scrabbling for toeholds, Mr Chester clambered over the wall.

Then it was Marjorie's turn. I showed her where to put her hands, and moved her feet for her, while Mr Chester leaned over the wall, stretching out desperately to grab her arm. Finally, he got hold of her wrist. 'Now you PUSH, Brianna,' he yelled, 'and I'll PULL.'

I set my shoulder under her ample backside as it rose up the wall, and shoved with all my might. Finally, thankfully, with a wail and a scraping, slithering sound, she disappeared from view. Then they both looked down at me, over the wall. For one crazy moment I entertained the notion of saying 'See y'around, folks,' and making a bolt for it, back the way we'd come. But I knew I couldn't. I started to climb up the wall, and as soon as he could reach, Mr Chester grabbed my arm and heaved. Quite a little crowd had gathered to watch as I coasted over the top of the wall, only slightly grazing my knee. A couple of lads broke into slow, sarcastic clapping.

I looked neither to left nor right as we walked away, smoothing down our clothes. We were all very subdued as we headed into the first café we came across and ordered some drinks.

Mr Chester was the first to recover his composure. 'Well,' he said cheerily, 'that was a bit of an adventure, wasn't it?'

A long silence followed this remark. Then Mrs Chester said, 'I think I'd like to go back now, dear.'

'Oh, but it's still early! I thought we might take in The Grand Master's Palace, and have another look at the harbour where the Colossus is supposed to have stood. Do you know about the Colossus, Brianna? And then . . .'

Mrs Chester shook her head. 'I'd like to go back.'

Long years of cohabitation with his wife must have made Mr Chester know when it was useless to try to push things. He shut up, a bit tight-lipped, and soon we were crawling back to Lindos in the hired car, eating the rest of the sandwiches. It was barely two in the afternoon.

When we got to the apartment I felt hot and dusty, and in desperate need of a swim. 'Look,' I announced, 'I'd love a dip. I'm just going to go down to the beach and . . .'

'Good idea,' said Mr Chester. 'I'll come with you. And while we're gone, Marjorie, why don't you have a little nap. Then we can have a nice evening together.'

It was like a life sentence. I couldn't get away from

them. At the beach, Mr Chester did fifteen minutes of energetic crawl across the bay and back, then sat and *waited* for me. I mean *waiting* was very obviously all he was doing. So after I'd suggested a couple of times that I'd be *fine* on my own, why didn't he head off back and I'd see him later, and he'd said, 'No problem, I'll wait,' I gave up and said I was ready to go.

Back at the apartment I stretched out on the terrace in the one patch of sun I could find to try and improve my tan. The terrace was every bit as hard and unyielding as the landing stage at *WATERWORLD*. As I shifted about trying to get comfortable I worked out that there were only four days of the holiday left, and I felt very sorry for myself.

Pandora !!! Just dashing this off as I wait for Alexander to finish work. We're going to go into Kalimaros to tour the discos tonight. He's a fabulous dancer. And tomorrow he's got A DAY OFF!! Bliss! He said he'd take me out on his bike and show me the real Rhodes that the tourists never see. I can't believe I'm going to have a whole day with only him. It's TOO MUCH!! Can't wait to show you his photo! ♡
Love, love, love, Zoë xxx

♥

Going Solo

I think being trapped between the fortification walls represented a bit of a turning point in the holiday as far as Mrs Chester was concerned. When she emerged from the master bedroom after her siesta she was quiet and peevish, as though she was tired of making an effort and wanted to let everyone know that this really wasn't her sort of holiday at all. It was late afternoon and a lovely, balmy breeze had sprung up, stirring all the plants on the terrace and making the vine canopy over the table sway wildly about. I leaned on the wall loving the feel of it on my face, but it didn't please Mrs Chester. She slammed back into her bedroom, and re-emerged with two bits of string. Then she got me to hold a chair for her while she caught up the hanging vines and tied them back in two bunches. Exactly like a pair of net curtains.

'Is there anything I can do, Mrs Chester?' I asked nervously, as she stamped into the kitchen.

She came out immediately with a little red plastic dustpan and brush and thrust it into my hands. 'Do you think you could give the terrace a sweep?' she asked. 'I do think all the leaves make it look so messy, don't you?'

I started crossing back and forth over the tiles in an uncomfortable, crouched position, scooping up all the leaves that had fallen. Meanwhile, Mr Chester had followed his wife into the kitchen and was arguing with her about going out that night. She wanted to stay in; he didn't.

'So a nice, simple spaghetti doesn't suit you, Derek?' she was saying, icily.

'I'm not saying that at all, Marjorie,' he replied. 'I just think you should take the night off after all that happened today. We could pop into Lindos and eat there.'

'With all those crowds and all those people getting drunk? I'd rather stay here, thank you.'

'Now, Marjorie. If we go in early, there won't be so many people about, will there?'

'There'll be enough.'

'Well, I just don't think you should cook tonight. You're on holiday, after all.'

'Yes, Derek. I *am* on holiday. I'm glad that fact hadn't escaped your notice,' she replied, in a voice throbbing with such fearful meaning that Mr Chester beat a hasty retreat and sat down heavily on one of the terrace chairs.

Bent double, I passed by him, still sweeping up leaves.

In the end, though, Mr Chester won and Mrs Chester agreed rather stiffly to a meal out that night. I had no option but to go out with them. When I desperately tried to say that I'd sooner stay here on my own, they were adamant.

'Not after dark, Brianna.'

'Not on your own.'

'That door has no real lock on it, Brianna.'

'Not on your own after dark.'

The three of us set off together at about seven. I'd almost forgotten Zoë had come on holiday with us by this stage. I felt as if I'd been in this threesome for eternity. The Chesters were sort of not speaking to each other, and the real reason for them insisting on me joining them dawned on me: I was needed as a sort of buffer zone between the two. Terrific.

As we got into the centre of Lindos, the little restaurants were just opening up and beginning to ply their trade. Mrs Chester wouldn't admit to liking the look of any of them. So we wandered round and round, and as it got later and later the streets began to fill up with people.

'You see?' she said, sniffily. 'I told you it would be crowded.'

Exhibiting masterful control, Mr Chester said nothing, but steered us into a back-street we'd not been down before. There was a tiny bistro right at the end, and on its doorstep sat an old woman, preparing something in a basin on her knee. She waved to us cheerfully and, as we drew closer, we could see what she was doing.

Shelling live snails.

Mrs Chester took one look at the black, splintered, squirming carnage and left, her hand pressed to her mouth. It seemed to confirm absolutely, completely, and for all time that she had been right to want to stay at home and eat a simple spaghetti.

She didn't say another word for the next forty minutes. Mr Chester started in with a lecture about how we shouldn't judge the culinary customs of other lands, but it fell on entirely deaf ears.

No one seemed to have much of an appetite after that. I certainly didn't. We ended up slinking into a straight pizza place, choking down a large, plain Margherita, and heading back home at some speed. And there, on my pillow, was a note from Zoë, folded into a tiny square.

> Hi Bri!!
> Going to be really late tonight.
> PLEASE PLEASE cover for me. I know
> you'll think of something. Just shout
> through the door that I'm asleep or
> something. LOADS 'O' LOVE. Zoë x
> P.S. DESTROY THIS NOTE!
> P.P.S. DO THE SAME FOR YOU WHEN
> YOU MEET SOMEONE!!!

I did manage to cover for Zoë that night, but I can't say I did it with a very good grace. I was cleaning my teeth at the basin after a midnight snack when Mr Chester tapped on the door and called softly, 'Zoë? Zoë? Was that you I heard moving about?'

'Yes, Daddy!' I carolled, through a mouthful of mint foam.

'You're back late, dear!'

'Shh, Daddy!' I gurgled. 'Brianna's asleep!'

And thankfully, that satisfied him.

I was beginning to forget what Zoë looked like. By the time I woke up the next day, she was dressed and shoving things in a little backpack, ready to go out again.

'Zoë?' I said sleepily. 'Zoë – you did come back last night, didn't you?'

'Yes, of course I did!' she squealed. 'What d'you take me for?'

'Someone who's gone brain-dead and obsessional,' I thought, as I asked, 'What time d'you get in?'

'Oh, about four.'

'*FOUR*! And you're going out already – it's only eight-thirty!'

'I don't need sleep,' she cried, bounding over and planting a kiss on the top of my head. 'I'm in love. We want to make the most of today. He's got the *day off*.' Then she stopped and looked at me. 'Bri, thanks for covering for me. I wish you could have met someone too.'

''S'OK,' I muttered. 'I just wish your parents would let me alone. I mean – they're being really kind and everything but . . .'

There was a *parp* from outside. Loverboy's motorbike. 'Must dash!' squealed Zoë, and fled.

Not long after that, I got up too. There was no sound from the Chesters' bedroom. I let myself out and wandered through the tiny streets into the centre of Lindos, trying to decide whether to go into one of the cafés and order breakfast. But I didn't have the heart for it, not on my own. So I bought three fat, hot croissants and headed back to the apartment. The croissants were a bit of a peace offering. When I got back, I was going to put my foot down. It was a matter of basic survival.

As I opened the front door, I could smell coffee. Mr Chester seemed almost overcome with gratitude at the sight of the croissants.

'Brianna – what a LOVELY idea!' he said. 'I'll just take one in to Marjorie with her coffee – she'll be so pleased! She doesn't sleep very well in this heat, you know. I told her to have a lie in.'

When he re-emerged from the bedroom, I told him about my plans to go to the beach. He was quite acquiescent. I think he knew it was time to give me some space.

'Yes, I think a QUIET day's on the agenda today,' he said. 'Well, not Zoë's agenda, anyway, ha ha. She told me about her plans.'

I smiled mirthlessly back at him, and he continued, 'Fine, Brianna, you go on down to the beach, and we'll see you later. As long as you're careful. Your parents have entrusted your care to us, and I don't take that responsibility lightly. So . . .' and he ran through his A-Z of nags once more.

It was such a relief to be on the beach on my own that for the first couple of hours I felt really quite happy. I hired a sunbed and soaked up the sun for a while, then I swam, sluiced off under the beach shower and

♥ 104 ♥

bought an ice-cream. I sat looking around me as I ate it. I couldn't see any of the people we'd got to know at the start of the holiday; they must have all flown home. Everyone seemed to be in couples or friendly groups – kissing, chatting, laughing, oiling each other – and suddenly I felt so alone it hurt.

I had the sun, the sea, the sand, but no one to share it with. I'd come to terms with the fact that a disastrous night with the beach vampires and a few disco-snogging sessions were going to be my lot as far as holiday romances went, but it would have been so good to spend some time with Zoë. With the *old* Zoë. When I wasn't feeling really angry with her for dumping me I could appreciate that she was smitten with Alexander, and almost understand why she was behaving like she was. But it didn't make it any easier to bear, or make me any less alone.

I was almost glad when Mr Chester appeared at my side to say he'd made a big salad for lunch, if I cared to join them. I really didn't think I could face eating solo at one of the beach restaurants.

The end of the holiday had been staring me in the face with the finality of death. Now it began to seem almost welcome. I realised, with some horror, that I *wanted* to go home.

Zoë and Alexander whirled back from their tour of the secret bits of Rhodes just as the sun was setting. They burst into the apartment, where the Chesters and I were sitting silently reading, radiating pleasure and happiness.

Zoë looks fantastic, I thought bitterly. I must look like an old cabbage in comparison. It's right what they say, about beauty coming from within. All I've got within me right now is resentment and depression. Whereas *she* . . .

'I've just come back to get changed for the evening!' carolled Zoë. 'Alexander wants to go to this special fish restaurant at Kalimaros . . .'

'Not many people know about it,' said Alexander, smugly. 'It's right on the quay; you watch the fishing boats come in by moonlight, then you eat the pick of the catch.'

'How wonderful,' enthused Mr Chester. 'Where did you say it was?'

Go on, Mr C., I thought cruelly, tell them you're going to go along too. But he didn't. He just listened as Alexander described it some more. And it all sounded so perfect I wanted to cry.

Soon afterwards, Zoë waved Alexander off, with lots of hand-kissing and promising to be back in an hour on his part. She wouldn't look at me as she rushed by to the bathroom. I was definitely in the role of someone you tried to avoid because you felt guilty about her. When she emerged from our bedroom half an hour later, looking stunning, Mrs Chester said quite firmly, 'Let's all have a little drink together, shall we?'

It was very wooden, sitting round the terrace table under the vine net curtains, sipping Pimms together. Zoë so much wanted to be somewhere else she seemed like a bird desperate to take flight. Her whole being was listening out for Alexander, though she did manage to turn to me and invite me once more to *WATERWORLD*, tomorrow. I once more very firmly turned it down. 'Look,' I announced to the table at large, 'it's great Zoë's met someone she's having such a ball with. But there's no way I'm tagging along. I'm OK, honestly.'

Zoë looked massively relieved and Mrs Chester leaned over and patted my hand. 'That's very understanding of you, dear,' she murmured.

'And it's just as well, too,' beamed Mr Chester. 'The tour representative told me about a little coach trip tomorrow, out to the ruins of Kamiros. And I've already booked three tickets!'

The coach trip wasn't too bad, mainly because I'd sort of given up inside and become numb to everything. I'd decided that was the most restful thing to do.

Kamiros was on the opposite coast to Lindos, on a cliff at the end of a long, hot, dusty road, and the coach driver-cum-guide was in a bad mood. When we got there he did little more than stomp off to buy a group ticket, tell us all to be back at the coach at four sharp, lay back in the driver's seat and go to sleep.

Mr Chester wasn't fazed by this disgraceful copping-out. He bought a guidebook, and slowly began to tour the chess-board ruins of the ancient town, reading aloud as he went. Soon he had not only Mrs Chester and me but half the bus following him. He warmed to his theme, explaining which bit of the three-tiered city was for commerce, which for residential use, which had sacred significance. At one point, he actually asked the crowd if there were any questions.

The glare of the white ruins began to give me a headache. I wandered away, and walked right to the edge of the cliff. The sky was so blue it defied belief, the sea glinting and just as blue beneath it, and hanging there, always, the white hot sun. I felt I could understand why the stories about the old Greek gods had been so extreme, so excessive. The landscape and the climate demanded it.

How can *anywhere* be this hot, I thought. It was like being blow-torched. Everything looked hazy, my eyes couldn't focus properly. I had to get into some shade. Desperately, I looked around me. There were three parched little trees at the top of the hill, just beyond all that was left of the temple of Athena. They weren't exactly shady elms, but they'd give a bit of shelter. Panting with every step, I dragged myself up towards them.

As I drew closer, I swore silently to myself. Someone had got there before me. A boy was sprawled there, leaning up against one of the tree-trunks, with his back to me.

Well, too bad, I thought, as I carried on towards the trees. This is no time for holding back and respecting other people's space. I'm about to die from sunstroke. I stopped a short distance from the boy and coughed, hopefully. 'Would you mind if I . . . ?'

The boy turned round. It was Karl.

♥

I'm No Princess

He looked at me, utterly gorgeous, totally unsmiling. 'Oh, it's you,' he said, unenthusiastically. 'Would I mind if you what?'

'If I shared your shade,' I said, heart pounding. 'Sorry, I didn't know it was *you*.'

'So you wouldn't have asked if you had known?'

'No, I didn't mean – oh *look*. I've got to get out of this *sun*.' And I threw myself down beside him. He hated me but I didn't care. I was too parched to care about anything.

'Don't get too near,' he said. 'I'm hot enough as it is.'

'Well, move over a bit then,' I snapped, and he did, very slightly.

'Better? It's not exactly cool under here.'

'Yes, better,' I murmured thankfully, as my eyes began to function again out of the glare. 'You don't know where you can get water round here, do you? I'm so thirsty I could . . .'

'God, any more requests? First she muscles in on my shade, then she wants my water.'

'I only asked where I could buy some . . .'

'There's no shop open. The last one closed down

two million years ago. Didn't you read the guide book?'

'Oh, ha ha.'

'Here,' he said, pulling a bottle out of his rucksack and handing it to me. 'Have some. If you don't mind drinking from the same bottle as me.'

Gratefully, I seized the bottle he held out, saying, 'I'm so thirsty I don't care *what*'s been drinking from – I mean . . .'

He smiled, wryly. 'That's all right then.'

'Thanks. This is great.' I took a long swig. 'Oooh, lovely.'

'Well, leave me a bit in the bottom.'

I screwed the top back on and handed the bottle back to him.

'So,' he said, 'all alone? Where's the princess?'

I gawped at him. 'How did *you* know she was called that?'

He laughed. 'I didn't. But the name does kind of spring to mind when you're around her.'

'She's not always that snotty,' I said loyally. 'Your mates were well out of order the other day, barging her off the landing stage like that.'

'That was an accident. And you knew it was, too.'

'Look, it wasn't me that got you banned!'

'No, but you didn't help!'

'Oh, knock it off. Look – I am really, really sorry you didn't get to have any more rides on that stupid banana. I realise it must have *ruined* your whole holiday and I *profoundly* apologise to you and all your friends. OK?'

There was a long silence. Then I sneaked a sideways look at him, and saw that he was trying not to grin. 'Where are your friends, anyway?' I said quickly. 'I thought you went round in a pack together?'

'Like jackels. No, not always. I've been spending some time on my own.'

'Why?'

'Why. Well, after a week or so of sinking ten pints of lager and then throwing up I just fancied bit of a break.'

For some reason, my insides had gone all warm. 'Why did you go on holiday with them,' I asked, 'if you didn't like their type of holiday?'

'What is this, an interrogation? Why did you go on holiday with the princess?'

'She's my good friend. And she asked me. I mean – I'd never get to go somewhere like this with my family.'

'Some friend,' he said. 'She's dumped you for that fascist water-sports guy, hasn't she?'

I gawped again. 'Have you been spying on us?'

He laughed. 'Come off it! I was out on the bike yesterday and I saw her in a bar – near Lardos Beach. She was with the guy from *WATERWORLD*. I bet he only banned us to impress her with how macho he is. The prat. Anyway, he seemed to fancy himself a lot more than he fancied her.'

I pulled a face. 'That figures. He's called Alexander, and he's Greek-Australian. Ego the size of – anyway, he's awful.'

'She didn't think so. She kept collapsing all over

him. Someone ought to tell her that if you act like a pushover you get treated like one.'

'She's in love!' I said indignantly.

'Oh, crap. He'll be off with another tourist next week. What a smarm merchant.'

There was a silence. Karl's views on Alexander matched mine so exactly I didn't know what to say. So I changed the subject. 'Why *did* you go on holiday with that lot?' I asked.

He turned towards me. 'Bit like you, I suppose. Opportunity. I play football with them, they're OK, we always have a laugh. I knew they had this holiday set up but I didn't want to be in on it. Then one of them dropped out – couldn't make the payments. They offered it to me cheap. I'm at college, I've got the whole summer off – so I did a bit of building site work and got the money together.'

'And now you're regretting it.'

'No. It's been OK. They're good mates. It's like I said – I just fancied some time on my own.'

'I don't blame you – that one with the stereo is brain dead,' I said, nastily.

'Oh, *cruel*! He really fancies you. He keeps going on about you, and what he'd like to – how much he likes you.'

Inside, I glowed. That kind of complement is always welcome, even from someone like Reg. 'He isn't exactly subtle, is he?' I said. 'Barging into Zoë. And he wouldn't let go of my arm for about ten minutes.'

'That's his pulling technique. He hasn't twigged yet

that it tends to send girls running in the other direction. He always goes for princess types, too, the poor sod, and he doesn't stand a chance.'

'Look – I'm not a princess,' I said, fervently. 'That's Zoë, and she only does it some of the time. I've got four brothers at home. You can't be a princess with four brothers.'

'Older or younger?'

'Both. Equal hell, both sides.'

He smiled at me, and I began to smile back. Then, somewhere at the edge of my consciousness, I heard a rumbling sound, and for some instinctive reason, it filled me with panic. I shot to my feet and peered down the hill towards the car park, shading my eyes. It was nearly empty – and heading off down the road, in a cloud of dust, I saw the rear end of our bus.

'Oh, no!' I wailed. 'Oh my *GOD!* That's the *BUS!* They've gone without me!'

♥

The Ride Of A Lifetime

Karl stood up next to me. 'What were you on, some kind of tour?'

'Yes! With Zoë's parents! I can't believe they've just gone off without . . .' I broke off and peered at my watch. 'Oh, God. It's 4.15. They told me the bus went at four. But they might have *looked* for me – or at least *shouted*.'

'Well, you're some way off, up here. Maybe they did look, but not this far.'

I gazed at Karl, panic rising. I felt completely abandoned.

'Why don't you go down to the ticket office and ask there,' he said. 'They might have left a message for you.'

I started to run down the hill, heedless of the heat and the thorny little plants snatching at my ankles. Without saying a word, Karl had started to run beside me. Once, when I stumbled, he put out his hand and caught me by the arm.

I raced down the main street of the ruined town, and across the stretch of gravel in the entranceway. I came to a crash landing against the side of the wooden ticket office and shouted through the hatch,

'Excuse me! That bus that left – was there a couple on there who . . . ?'

'Ah,' said the ticket man importantly. 'You are Miss Brianna? Yes? From England?'

'Yes!' I wailed.

'Your guardian left message. He very angry, very worried, very anxious. His wife ill – heat-stroke. He take her back, and come back here with taxi for you. He say wait here.'

I heaved a sigh of relief. But I didn't like the sound of that 'very angry, very worried, very anxious'. I bet he was spitting teeth.

I turned to Karl. 'I,' I announced, 'am in *big* trouble,'

'I can give you a lift,' said Karl, shrugging. 'Get you back to Lindos before the bus gets there. Then at least the old man won't have to fork out for a taxi.'

'Oh – *could* you?' I'd come over totally trembly. And not with the thought of avoiding Mr Chester's wrath, either. 'That would be *brilliant*. You'd save my life – you'd—'

'OK,' he said. 'Don't overdo it. Come on.'

His bike was parked in the little car-park behind the ticket office. 'Here it is,' he said. 'These Greek bikes are pretty sad, really. Real slow. You should see what I've got at home.'

Love to, I thought. He straddled the bike, and kicked the engine into life. 'Come on,' he shouted to me over the engine roar. 'Get on.'

So, as elegantly as I could, I climbed on behind him.

'Now hold *on*,' he shouted, as he started to leg the bike forward. 'It's real bumpy here.'

I had no choice. The first lurch threw me right backwards, so I was forced to hold on to him really tightly. Then we were off.

It was on the bike ride that I became seriously smitten with Karl. I wrapped myself round him as close as I could get, pressing my face into his back, breathing in the smell of his sun-bleached shirt. My legs were against his legs, and my arms were around his chest. We roared along, faster and faster, just him and me in this wind tunnel on the edge of the white cliff tops, and I could feel every muscle move as he manoeuvred the bike.

I just about passed out with it all, I can tell you.

After a while, Karl turned sideways towards me, so that his mouth was like two centimetres away from mine, and started to say something. And the great thing was, I had to get even nearer to his mouth to hear what it was.

'Look – there's the bus. We've caught up with it already. I'll see if I can get the driver's attention – then we can get you on board.'

It was as if he'd hit me. The last thing I wanted to do was get on that stupid bus! I wanted to go on riding behind him for ever. But Karl had overtaken the bus, and was making vague 'stop' signs with his left arm. Then he slowed down until he was parallel to the bus driver's cabin, and made some more signs. Then all of a sudden he accelerated away, leaving the bus behind, his bike eating up the road as if it was ravenous.

After a while he slowed down again, turned his gorgeous profile to me again, and said, 'I couldn't get him to stop. The driver must think I'm a highwayman or something – he was swearing at me to clear off.' Then he faced the front and we accelerated off again.

I wrapped my arms tighter round his back, and let my face rest blissfully against his shoulder. This kind of glow was spreading all through me. Because I'd seen the driver's face too, and he hadn't been swearing at all. He hadn't needed to – he hadn't noticed Karl's signals. Because – I realised in delight – Karl hadn't been trying very hard to *get* noticed.

It's Better With Two

We drove off round the coast road, through a few straggling seaside resorts, and into the centre of a really pretty little village. When we reached the village square, all laid out with benches and well-watered trees, Karl slowed the bike and stopped.

'Look,' he said, turning back towards me, 'at this rate we'll be back hours before that bus. They always make loads of stops to drop all the punters off. And I could murder a drink, seeing as you finished off my water.'

'I'd love a drink,' I said, climbing off the bike. 'Where?'

'There,' he said, pointing. 'I've been to that bar before. It's good.'

Good? It was fantastic – the sort of Greek-atmospheric place I'd dreamed of finding. We climbed up the steps to the veranda and sat down opposite each other at an old wooden table. All along the veranda edge, lush, big-leaved plants tumbled out of white-painted oil drums; over our heads the vine sun-shade swayed in the breeze.

The friendly owner bought us bottles of beer and water, and we sat there savouring the cold drinks, chatting about this and that, and laughing over me being left behind by the bus. Karl had a wonderful laugh, sort of slow to get going, then really deep and warm. Laughing made his whole face come alive. I tried to seem dead relaxed as I chatted, but I felt like every particle in me was on full alert. All I wanted to do was watch him, but my eyes kept sliding away from his.

After a while, there was a stretch of silence. I looked over the top of my glass to see Karl staring at me, looking as though he was working something out.

'What?' I said, defensively.

'I was just thinking about that stuff your friend came out with, about how we were gits and pathetic and . . .'

'Look – you've got to realise how . . . threatening you lot seemed.'

'Did you feel threatened, too?'

'Well – a bit. I mean – there were seven of you. And two of us.'

'Two's enough, I can tell you! Just two is scary enough.'

'Oh, charming. What d'you mean?'

'I mean the way you look at people – and laugh together – like you're judging every bloke that walks past.'

Well, we are, I thought. 'Aren't you doing that to every girl?' I asked.

'I dunno – it's different.'

'Yeah? Why?'

'It just is. We don't do it – so seriously.'

There was a pause. He's shy, I thought in sudden delight. Someone this lush is actually a bit shy.

The sun was slowly going down in the sky; everything glowed red in its light. Then, as if at a signal, hundreds of cicadas began to chirp in a nearby tree. 'This is wonderful,' I sighed. 'When did you discover it? Not your mates' sort of hang-out, is it?'

He grinned at me. 'Look, Brianna, I am not joined to them by the hip. I told you, I've been spending some time on my own. I came here last night.'

'It's OK for blokes,' I said, 'they can go into bars on their own.'

'Yeah, but it's not as good as when you're . . .'

'With your mates?'

'With someone. Let's go.'

Back on the bike, I saw the approach of Lindos with a sinking heart. Now I had to face Mr Chester, and I had to say goodbye to Karl. Unless . . .

Karl locked his bike up when we got off it. 'I'll come in with you,' he said. 'Maybe it'll smooth things over if he sees someone's seen you right home.'

Somehow, I doubted it. What Mr Chester would see was one of the louts from the airport with a fast bike. Still, it kept Karl by my side for a bit longer. And that was beginning to matter more than any row with Zoë's dad.

I opened the door and called softly, 'Mr Chester? Hi? I'm back!'

Mr Chester came out of the main bedroom at speed,

a finger clamped to his lips. 'Don't wake her!' he hissed. 'She's been in a terrible state!'

'I'm back,' I repeated. I thought I should repeat it. Maybe he'd forgotten he'd abandoned me in a prehistoric town.

'Thank GOODNESS!' he said. 'We were SO worried, leaving you like that. I was just about to call a taxi to go back.'

'I'm really sorry about missing the bus.'

'After I'd TOLD you four o'clock latest! The driver refused to wait beyond 4.15. But how on earth did you get back so soon . . . ?'

Karl stepped forward. 'Hi,' he said. 'I gave Brianna a lift. We bumped into each other by the temple. I guess that's why she didn't hear you shout for her.'

'I shouted for AGES!' said Mr Chester, almost plaintively. 'And I went round all the streets again, and up to the temple – where were you?'

'In the shade, under some trees,' I explained. 'The heat had made me really . . .'

'Well, that's what happened to Marjorie,' he broke in. 'She was in such a state. Otherwise I wouldn't have dreamed of just going off without you and leaving you ON YOUR OWN . . .'

This was priceless. Mr Chester really felt the need to justify what he'd done.

'Marjorie gets very bad, sometimes,' he went on. 'I couldn't let her travel back on her own. I know it sound silly but – she needs me at those times.'

There was an awkward silence, and then Karl said, 'Well – Brianna didn't come to any harm. Luckily.'

'No,' said Mr Chester. 'Er – thank you.'

There was a muffled sort of wail from the main bedroom, like a seal being suffocated. 'There's Marjorie,' said Mr Chester weakly. 'I'd better go in to her – tell her you're safe.'

He disappeared, and Karl and I were left standing on the terrace alone. It was almost dark now, and a soft, warm wind had begun to blow, stirring the vine leaves.

'I love this weather,' said Karl. 'The nights are the best. Where does that wind come from?'

'I don't know,' I said, 'but it's magic.'

There was a pause, and then Karl muttered, 'Well – I'd better go.'

'Let me buy you a drink,' I said in a rush. 'To say thank you. Or dinner. To really say thank you. I mean – you saved my life, today. And I'm starving. Aren't you? We could walk into Lindos – there's lots of nice places to eat . . .'

'All right, all right,' he said, grinning. 'I'm convinced. Come on then.'

♥

The Nights Are The Best

I tiptoed over to the Chesters' bedroom, and poked my head round the door.

'Mr Chester,' I whispered. He was sitting by Mrs Chester on the bed, mopping her forehead with a wet flannel. 'Is it OK if I go out for a few hours? Just into Lindos. To get something to eat with Karl.'

He looked round distractedly. 'To eat? Yes, of course. Here . . .' He drew something out of his pocket. 'On me.' And he handed me a little roll of bank notes.

I was stunned. 'Oh, you don't have to . . .' I began, but he'd put his finger to his lips again, smiling, so I just crept out.

Karl was standing on the terrace with his back to me, looking out to the shoreline over the low stone wall. I had this overwhelming urge to go and wrap my arms round him again and rest my face against his shoulders, just like on the bike.

'Karl!' I hissed. 'Look!' I waved the money at him. 'Courtesy of Mr Chester!'

'Great! He's got a guilty conscience, has he? Let's go.'

'Give me *three* minutes,' I said, and shot into my bedroom.

I grabbed my hairbrush and painfully began to put right the havoc from the bike ride. Then I zipped on some lippy and mascara, and a bit of damage-limitation aftersun cream. My tan is really beginning to look good, I thought, as I stood in front of the mirror. I turned, torn with indecision, to the wardrobe. God forbid that I should look as if I was *trying too hard* . . .

Oh, sod it. This was Greece. This was my holiday. And this was by far the best reason I'd had so far to wear my red dress. And if Zoë had chosen that night to borrow it I'd – well, she'd just better not have, that's all.

Five minutes later, I was at Karl's side again. In red.

'Blimey,' he said. 'You've changed – in three minutes. I didn't think that was possible for a girl.'

'Don't make sexist comments,' I retorted.

'OK. You look great. Is that sexist?'

I laughed. 'Let's go.'

We clattered down the worn stone steps together and off along the narrow street. Already the place was filling up with people planning to have a great night out. Swimsuits and shorts had been swapped for cutaway dresses and spiky heels, and there was a sense of excitement everywhere.

The lanes were crowded so we walked close together to let people get by. My hand was hanging by my side, swinging, awkward, unattached. What it wanted to do more than anything in the world was hold his.

'Let's go in here,' I said, stopping by a wide,

impressive doorway. 'My favourite bar.' It was the swankest place I could think of. Zoë and I had only been in it twice – we felt a bit intimidated by it.

We walked through all the potted palms and painted wooden parrots up to the bar. I studied Karl as he stood there, ordering drinks. He really was something special. Short, soft brown hair. And beautiful eyes. And long legs. And a wonderful mouth. And –

'Where d'you want to eat?' he said.

'On a rooftop,' I answered, without thinking.

'All right, princess! Where?'

'I am not a princess. There are loads of rooftop restaurants here. They're great. You're right near the sky and there's a terrific view and . . .'

'You've convinced me. Come on, let's find some-where to sit.'

This bar was so posh it had sofas rather than stools to sit on. We found an empty one and sank into it. He sat close to me, but it might not have meant anything. It could have been just to leave room for someone to sit at the other end. He could just see me as a mate, someone he'd rescued. It's not as though we're on a date, I thought. But if this evening ends with him just saying 'Bye, thanks for the meal' and me saying 'Bye, thanks for the lift,' I think I'll kill myself.

We both took a few sips of our drinks in silence. I stared at his hand as he picked up his glass. I watched his throat as he swallowed. Come on, this is the age of sexual equality, I told myself. Launch yourself on him. But somehow, I couldn't.

We finished our drinks quickly, hardly talking, and

then went off to find a rooftop restaurant. The first two we tried were full, then the third said they could fit us in in ten minutes or so.

'Why don't have a drink while you wait, sir and madam?' said the waiter, indicating a tiny bar made of sherry barrels.

We bought drinks, and stood in the corner, under an indoor tree that twinkled with fairy lights. We were the only people waiting there. Waiting, waiting. I couldn't think of a thing to say. I couldn't even look at his face, so I stared at his chest. All I wanted to do was kiss him. It was getting unbearable.

He took a long swig of beer, and put his glass down. I put my drink on the bar too. Then I took a deep breath, moved closer to him, and laid one hand flat on his chest. 'Karl—' I began.

It was like I'd pulled a mains switch. He grabbed hold of my hand, wrapped his other arm round my back, and pulled me in close. Then we were kissing in a way that made all the other kissing I'd done in my life seem like kids' stuff.

After a while I drew back and looked up at him, and he looked back. Then I pulled his head down to mine again.

When we came up for air, the waiter was hovering nearby. 'I – er – had to give your table to someone else,' he said, a little stiffly. 'But there'll be another one free in a few minutes.'

Karl looked at me, hugging me tight, then we both started laughing.

♥

Until Tomorrow

Once we were seated at our little table in the corner on the rooftop, we both moved in as close to each other as we could. He'd trapped one of my legs between his under the table, and on top I'd captured both his hands beneath mine. The magic wind was still blowing, making the candles stream sideways, bringing the scent of jasmine with it. And I was shaking. I couldn't believe what had just happened – what was still happening.

'Look at that sky,' I said. 'Wasn't I right to want a rooftop?'

'Yes. Are those really the same stars we see in the boring old UK?'

'No, special Greek ones.'

'Hey, Brianna,' he said, grinning. 'That was – I thought I was going to get a smack in the face back then. When I grabbed you.'

'Oh, for heaven's sake. Why d'you think I asked you out to eat?'

'To thank me, like you said. You'd've done it for anyone.'

'Oh no, I wouldn't. God, Karl, why are blokes so bad at body language? I haven't exactly been freezing you off since the bike ride, have I?'

He shook his head, happily. 'Maybe not – but after all that crap at Faliraki – I thought you thought we were all idiots.'

'Zoë thought that. I didn't. I just didn't have the guts to stand up to that greasy git Alexander. Anyway – what was I supposed to say? Don't ban the one in the green shorts, 'cos I fancy him?'

'Yeah! Why not?'

We laughed, and the waiter came and we ordered, garlic bread and steak and mushrooms and pasta – stuff that we liked, even if it didn't all go together. Then we settled to eating, stealing bits off each other's plates, and staring at one another across the table as we chewed.

'So,' Karl said, swallowing, 'Did you ever get to go on the banana?'

'No. And I don't want to.'

'Yeah, you do. We found somewhere else that has one. Stuff *WATERWORLD*. I could take you. Tomorrow.'

'Oh, great. So I have to face all your mates, do I, and have them bribe the boat driver to go extra fast to throw me off and . . .'

'Hang on, hang on, I didn't say anything about them coming along. We can hire it just for the two of us. That way it'll go even faster.'

'Oh, terrific. I've got a better idea. Let's just go to a beach – and do nothing.'

He smiled, widely. 'Almost nothing, maybe.'

We carried on eating, more slowly this time because we were holding hands and could only use our forks and fingers. 'Now let's go and get ice-cream on the beach,' Karl said, as we wiped our plates clean.

'You're mad! Nowhere will be open!'

'Yes it will. I know a really good . . .'

'Bar. You would. Let's go.'

This time we were so wrapped round each other as we went through the narrow stone streets we had difficulty walking. It was slow going, especially as we kept stopping to kiss. We made our way down to the shore, a way I'd never been before, and I began to hear music above the waves. And there, tucked beneath the cliff, was a fantastic café, full of welcoming, coloured lights and packed with people.

In no time we were nestled together at a little table, sharing Italian ice-cream.

'There's only two days of this holiday left,' I said mournfully.

'I know. Think of all the time we've wasted. If you hadn't been such a princess that day in Faliraki, we could've got it together then.'

'*ME*? It's *my* fault is it? You and your mates come on like some kind of rugby scrum – anyway, you were as bad. You looked at me like you hated me at Kamiros, when I tried to share your shade.'

'Tried to share? I don't remember getting a choice! And I only looked at you like that because I thought you hated me.'

'Well – I didn't.'

'And I didn't hate you.' He leaned over the table towards me, his mouth so close it gave me goosebumps. 'I fancied you something chronic. Nearly as much as I fancy you now.'

I sighed blissfully, and scooped the last of the fudge sauce from the bottom of the glass.

'In fact . . .' he went on, still halfway over the table, 'I fancied you from the plane.'

'Me too,' I said. 'Why didn't we do something about it *then*?'

'Well, it was all a bit crowded, remember? And besides, Reg really had something going for you. He – oh, God. I'd forgotten about Reg. He's going to go ballistic when he finds out I've got off with you.'

'So don't tell him.'

'No, I'll tell him he didn't stand a chance with you. Then it'll be all right.'

I shook my head over the male psyche. 'Why will that make it all right? I'd be gutted if someone said that to me.'

'Because if he didn't stand a chance, I didn't ruin anything for him.'

'I see. I think.'

We walked the long way back across the beach, stopping every now and then to kiss, then we lay down for a while in the sand, wound round each other, listening to the sighing of the waves. It occurred to me that with some other blokes, lying here so far away from anyone, I might feel a bit nervous. But somehow I didn't, with Karl. This time he could read my body language perfectly.

'I love the way your hair's all soft at the back of

your head,' I said, pushing my fingers into it. 'It looks spiky, but it's soft. Like a sea anemone.'

'A *sea anemone*? Is that meant to be a compliment?'

'Yes.'

'Well, yours looks like overdone candyfloss. What does it taste like?' And he caught a big strand of it between his teeth.

I laughed, and raised myself up on one elbow, so that I could stroke his hair and examine every inch of his face, before I kissed him again.

After a while he murmured, 'Brianna, I hate to bring this up. I'd like to lie here all night. But are you supposed to be back at any time?'

In panic, I looked at my watch. 'Oh, no. It's after *two*! Zoë's dad will go *spare*. That's twice in one day I've gone missing.'

He stood up and pulled me to my feet. 'Come on, we'll be back in ten minutes. And my bike's parked near your apartment, so he'll know you're still with me.'

'I'm not sure that'll reassure him,' I said. 'With any luck, Zoë will have covered for me. I've told enough lies about her and her precious Alexander this week. I even pretended to *be* her, once.'

Karl looked at me, amazed. 'How did you manage to do that?'

'I called out "Goodnight Daddy" while I was cleaning my teeth. He bought it.'

'God, girls are appalling. So . . . *devious*. How will I ever be sure you're telling me the truth?'

I laughed. 'Body language,' I said.

Too soon we were standing beside Karl's bike. 'Well, I'd better get back to Faliraki,' he said. 'Coming with me?'

I could tell he didn't mean it. Trying it on was kind of obligatory for a lad. 'No way,' I said. 'I bet you share a bedroom with at least two of the others, and you all snore.'

He laughed, and hugged me. 'So when can I see you tomorrow?' he asked.

Tomorrow. We had all of tomorrow. No school, no college, nothing to do but be together. 'As early as you like,' I said.

'Right. I'll pick you up for breakfast. If I have to watch Reg and the others eat one more full-fried-English, I'll go mental.'

'Fried breakfast,' I said. 'In this heat. How gross. I have cappuccino and croissants, and the occasional fresh fig.'

'OK, princess, whatever you say,' he grinned, and bent down to kiss me one last lovely time. Then he was on his bike and off into the night.

I watched him until he swerved round a corner and out of sight, then I floated up the stone steps and let myself through the main door. I tiptoed across the terrace. As I passed the vine net-curtains, I reached up and pulled the end of one of the bows. I just couldn't stop myself. The vine ropes tumbled down, chaotic and green and beautiful.

I crept into the bedroom. And there was Zoë, sitting up in bed, an indignant look on her face.

'It's *three o'clock*, Brianna! Where have you *been*? I got back early to *talk* to you.'

♥ 132 ♥

Well, excuse *me* for having my own *life*, I thought.

'I covered for you, anyway,' she went on. 'I said you were undressing.'

'Thanks, Zoë. I didn't realise it had got that late.' Actually, come to think of it, I didn't care.

'So – what were you up to?' she went on.

I told her, and I shall never forget the look on her face as I did.

Pandora & You will not BELIEVE what's happened! Brianna has got off with one of the LADS FROM HELL!! I know she likes roughing it but this is ridiculous. He's one of a group of morons who THREW me of a pier into the sea! I'm sure she's not safe with him. Still, she's probably only doing this because I've spent so much time with Alexander. I feel really responsible. Love Zoë xxxx

♥

Simply The Best

I woke up the next morning early, absolutely shot through with happiness. I couldn't believe how well things had turned out. Karl and I might only have two days left together but I wasn't going to let that depress me. I resolved they'd be the best two days ever.

I left Zoë asleep and raced into the bathroom. If I was going out with Karl for breakfast I needed a bit of preparation. I had a quick shower, hair wash, and squirted on lots of body cream. Then I put on my favourite shorts and T-shirt, and packed my cozzie, makeup and money into my little backpack. I wasn't planning on returning to the apartment until nightfall at the earliest.

Zoë had just staggered out of bed onto the terrace when there was a 'parp' from outside. It was recognisably not from Alexander's bike. I rushed to the wall, leaned over, and saw Karl, looking completely gorgeous with his hair all blown back from the bike ride, smiling up at me. I melted, waved, and rushed for the door.

'Brianna!' Zoë wailed. 'Are you off already? Can't we *talk*?'

I turned to her. 'No, Zoë, we can't. I'm off out.

With Karl. Tell your mum and dad, will you?' And I left.

Karl was locking up the bike when I ran down the steps. He turned, and we faced each other for a minute, a bit uncertain, then I walked forward and put both my arms round his neck. He looked down at me, laughing, and said, 'You always this forthright?'

'Yup. Making up for lost time,' I replied.

'Good,' he said, and we had a long, long kiss.

Breakfast was beautiful. Hot croissants, hot coffee, even fresh figs, just as I'd said. Karl lowered the tone a bit by having scrambled eggs too, but he said he felt really hungry. There was this incredible feeling of excitement between us. We talked and joked – we were so open together, as though we'd known each other for ages. And as though we knew there was no time to waste in playing mind games.

Lindos seemed different now I was with Karl. Every little thing gave us a buzz. We wrapped our arms round each other and walked slowly through the tiny streets, stopping to laugh at some appalling postcards, or admire some beautiful silver jewellery, or stroke a thin stray cat.

We headed for the same beach we'd been to last night and hired sunbeds and an umbrella. Holidays kind of accelerate intimacy. I oiled Karl's back, slowly and enjoyably, then he did mine.

'You don't go in for this topless thing, then?' he asked casually, as two particularly well-endowed girls walked by.

I looked him straight in the eye. 'No,' I said. 'I burn easily.'

For the next few hours we were just like all the other besotted couples on the beach, the ones I'd spent the last week envying so much. We held hands across the gap between the sunbeds as we talked together, comparing notes on the most embarrassing bits of our holidays so far. I won, of course. No amount of crass laddish behaviour on the part of Karl's friends could come near making up a threesome with Ma and Pa Chester. Then he told me he knew a bit about reflexology and gave me a foot massage, from which it was obvious he knew nothing about reflexology or massage, but it was still nice. After that he came and squeezed on my sunbed with me for a while, and we necked shamelessly; then – when we both fell off the sunbed onto the sand – we went for a swim.

We played around in the shallows for a while, splashing and giving each other piggy backs and falling backwards. Then we swam out to sea. It was silent and beautiful far out in the bay. We hung there, treading water. You can kiss really well while you're treading water. Just your mouths touching.

After a while we swam to some deserted rocks, clambered out and sunbathed with the surf crashing about us, until our hunger and the burning heat told us it was time to find somewhere shady for lunch.

'What d'you want to do later on?' he said, as we broke bits of rough Greek bread at a shabby little beach café. 'Take the bike out somewhere?'

'Yes,' I said greedily. 'Where?' I wanted to do everything, I wanted to fit it all in today.

'Up into the hills – see the countryside. It's great by bike. We can watch the sun go down from a mountain top.'

We went and lounged on our sunbeds on the shoreline for a couple more hours, then we had one last, lazy swim. As the sun got lower in the sky, we grew restless and headed back to Lindos to get the bike.

'You don't need to go in for anything do you?' said Karl, reluctantly, as we got near to the apartment.

I laughed. 'You mean shower, change, curl my hair? You think I need it?'

'No. You look gorgeous.'

'Well, let's go then.' And as I climbed on the bike behind him, I *felt* gorgeous, too. After a day like I'd had, anyone would.

I wrapped my arms tight round him and snuggled my face into his shirt. 'Quick, get going,' I said into the back of his neck. 'Before the Chesters see us and force us to go up and join them for a drink.'

At that he accelerated away so fast I was nearly thrown off backwards. We raced higher and higher up into the hills, past parched looking fields and rocky outcrops. Half the time I was admiring the landscape, the other half I spent admiring the way the muscles in Karl's back worked as he manoeuvred the bike round the tight bends. I couldn't seem to keep my hands still on his shoulders.

After a while he pulled up next to a little roadside

stall and bought a bottle of water, and we both had a long drink. Then we kissed, mouths cold at first from the water we'd drunk, and roared off again.

After about an hour it seemed as if we'd gone as high as we could go. We were right at the edge of a cliff, with a spectacular view out over the sea. Karl stopped the bike and swivelled round, swinging both legs over on top of mine. I laughed as I ducked back to avoid him cracking me one with his knee then I moved in even closer to him, put my arms round his waist, and kissed him.

'This is an amazing place, Karl,' I said, looking around.

'I know.'

'That view is – stunning!'

'Sod the view,' he said, and started kissing me.

After a while we climbed off the bike and lay on the grass and talked and necked some more, totally engrossed in each other. We stayed there until it got quite dark. I began to feel I didn't want to see anyone else, or speak to anyone else. Only Karl.

'Where d'you come from?' he asked suddenly. 'I mean – back home?'

I told him, and he told me where he lived. He said it was very rural, hard to get to. There was a silence as we both took in quite how far apart we lived, and quite how difficult it would be to see each other once we got home.

'Well, I've got the bike,' he said, after a while. 'I travel huge distances on that thing. I mean, I do thirty miles a day just to get to college.'

'Which one d'you go to?' I asked.

'Rochester Tertiary. Near Bedford.'

I felt as though the air around me was suddenly fizzing with static. 'Rochester Tertiary – on Rochester Street?' I said, breathlessly. 'By the station? Near the hospital?'

He stared at me. 'Yes. Brianna? Which one are . . .'

'*THAT'S WHERE I'M GOING!!*' I screamed, and threw myself on top of him.

♥

Unbelievable

It took us another five minutes before we really allowed ourselves to accept that we were going to the same college. Superstitiously, we checked the name of the principal, the number of dining rooms, the colour of the main building outside. Then we allowed ourselves to really celebrate.

'But won't you *mind?*' I squawked. 'I mean – are you sure you really *want* me there? You've probably got loads of girls in your class you fancy . . . you've probably . . .'

'Brianna, I'm doing an *engineering* course. There are only two other girls on it. And they're not my type.'

'Oh, this is brilliant. I'll be able to see *so much* of you . . .'

'Aren't you afraid I'll cramp *your* style? All those spunky new kids – all waiting to meet someone like you . . .'

I pulled a face at him. 'I've been to the college open day, remember. Studs were pretty thin on the ground, I can tell you.'

'That,' he said, stroking my hair back from my face, 'is great news. I don't want any competition. Not for you.'

I rolled over on to my back and stared up at all the impossibly bright stars and thought about the future. I'd put it out of my mind up until now, because it involved work, and effort, and change, all the things I didn't want to face until well after the holiday. But now the future had some kind of shape to it. It could be looked at, even looked forward to. The future had Karl in it.

So did the present.

Later, hunger and the desire for a drink made us mount the bike once more and head off into the night. We found a tiny, brightly lit restaurant, right off the beaten track, and peered in through the window. It was mostly full of locals but there were a few tourists round the edges, all looking superior because they'd found somewhere 'authentic'. Hungrily, I scanned the menu displayed at the front.

'Karl, let's go in – this looks great! All that mountain air has done me in – I'm famished.'

Karl looked worried. 'Er – Brianna – it's right at the end of the holiday and I'm, er . . .'

'Broke?'

'I'm afraid so.'

'Well I'm not. I'm loaded. The one good thing about being bored witless with the Chesters is you hardly spend any money. Come on.'

'Look – I can't let you pay for me.'

'Fine. Come in and watch me stuff my face and starve then. Come ON, Karl! You can buy me lunch at college!'

That convinced him. We ordered and ate slowly, in friendly silence, holding hands across the table. Then we drove back to Lindos. When Karl drew up outside the apartment, I was half asleep against his back.

'I'm nor gerring off,' I mumbled into his shirt.

'You what?'

'Can't move. Sleeping here.'

'OK, princess. Whatever you say,' he said, twisting round to rub his cheek against the top of my head. Then, after a few minutes, he said, 'Come on, Brianna. Move. It's our last day tomorrow, and I'm coming to pick you up at 6am.'

'OK,' I agreed happily, then I slid off, kissed him goodbye, and crawled up the steps to the apartment.

Zoë was fast asleep when I crept into our room. I was very, very careful not to wake her.

Dear Pandora ❤ It's past one o'clock and Brianna is still out with the git who threw me off the pier. I'm really worried. She wouldn't talk to me about him this morning - just raced off when she heard his bike. I just don't want her to get hurt. So much for keeping holiday romances in perspective! Not that I can talk!! See you soon ❤
xxx Zoë

♥

Head For The Hills

I didn't really expect Karl at six the next day, but I did wake up early. Zoë, however, had beaten me to it. She'd even made me a cup of tea.

'So – how's Karl?' she said, perching beside me on the bed.

'Fabulous. Much better without his mates. How's Alexander?'

'OK.'

'Only OK? When are you seeing him?'

'Not till later today. Bri, he's –'

'What?'

'He's really been putting the pressure on. For me to – you know.'

'Oh God. Sleep with him.'

She nodded, eyes downcast, and there was a silence. Then she went on, 'He said if I really loved him I – oh, OK, Bri. I know what you're thinking. And don't worry, I'm not going to. But when we're together, and he's . . . oh, I don't know. At the start of the holiday, he kept saying how he'd come to England to see me – he has an uncle there and everything – but . . . but he hasn't been saying that so much, and he's . . .' She broke off, and sighed.

'This really isn't just a holiday romance for you, is it Zoë?'

She shook her head. 'What about Karl?'

'Well, I . . . I don't know.' I didn't want to tell her he'd be at college with me next term. I didn't think it would exactly cheer her up.

I knew she wanted to talk more, but I felt driven – as driven as she'd been those first days with Alexander. It was my last day in Greece with Karl. And no one was going to shorten it for me, not if I could help it. I got up and got dressed, and soon after that Karl drew up outside. As we walked into Lindos, hand in hand, I told him it looked like he'd been right about Alexander.

'I think Zoë knows it too,' I said, 'she seemed really down, she wanted to talk, but I . . .'

'She'll get over him,' said Karl. 'He's a loser.'

'I know. I still can't believe she swallowed all his *spiel*. I mean – single red roses and stuff. Really, a girl's a lot better off with someone totally unromantic and practical. Like you.'

He stopped dead, and looked at me. 'You,' he said impressively, 'are going to eat your words in a minute.' Then he pulled a little white box out of his back pocket, and handed it to me.

Intrigued, I opened it. Inside was one of the thin silver bracelets we'd been admiring yesterday. 'Oh, *Karl* . . .' I began.

'*And* I had to knock the shop up to buy it this morning. Romantic or *what*?'

'But you're *broke* . . .'

'Reg owed me some money. I got it back last night. I had to threaten to trash his CD collection, but it worked.'

'That,' I said, slipping the bracelet onto my wrist, 'is probably the most romantic thing I've ever heard. *Thank* you, Karl – it's lovely. Doesn't silver look good on brown?'

'Beautiful,' he answered, and we wandered down to the beach.

That day followed the same lovely pattern as the day before. Even knowing we had to fly home the next day couldn't spoil it – it only seemed to make the time more precious. As we lay on the shoreline, letting the waves lap at us, Karl said we should do something really good tonight, something to mark the last night.

'Great,' I answered. 'Like what?'

'Well – I'd like to drive out to the hills, like we did last night. I can't think of anything better.'

I smiled at him. 'Me neither.'

'And this time dinner's on me.'

I laughed. 'Reg owed you that much did he?'

'Yup. But first – would you – could you bear it if . . .' He took a deep breath. 'There's a disco tonight at the hotel block we're staying in. Sort of last night bash. They've been making a really big deal of it.'

'Oh.'

'The guys have been on at me to go. 'Cos it's the last night of our holiday. They said I should bring you too. I thought if we just went for an hour or so . . .'

I put my arms round his neck and hugged him. 'Course we can go. I just – I was just thinking about Zoë. I wonder what's going to happen with Alexander tonight.'

'You could always bring her to the disco.'

'Somehow – *somehow* I think she'd turn that down. And Karl . . .'

'Yes?'

'If we're going to a disco, I need to go back to the flat. To change.'

'How long'll you take?'

'Just long enough for you to meet Ma and Pa Chester.'

'Oh, spare me,' he said. 'I'll sit outside on the bike.'

He did, too. I raced inside the apartment while he stretched out full length on the bike seats and shut his eyes. He needn't have worried, though. The place was empty. I think Ma and Pa Chester had given up checking up on us at this stage. And, as Zoë wasn't there, this time there was no contest for the white dress.

I showered and changed at top speed, then went wild with my eye-makeup, and rushed out to Karl. My hair was still dripping but I reckoned motorbikes make great hair dryers.

Karl smiled when he saw me. 'You look terrific,' he said. 'Go on – get on.'

I held on with one hand this time, and raked through

my hair with the other one as we sped along in the warm breeze. When we arrived, the hotel was already humming with life, and huge bundles of shiny balloons were tied all over the place.

'It's all part of their promotional budget,' Karl said. 'Send the punters off with a great night and they'll think the whole holiday was like that and come back for more.'

We met Karl's friends in the bar. I felt quite nervous walking over to them, but I needn't have worried. There were two other girls hanging out with them, so it wasn't like I was unique.

Reg took one look at me and groaned out loud. 'You look really gorgeous,' he said, sounding depressed. 'Karl, you're dead.'

And then the evening got going. Karl showed me round the pool and the gardens with their battered looking palm trees, and we found this old wooden bench behind some spiky bushes, really secluded. We stayed there for a while, arms round each other, just talking, then we started kissing. After a while we realised it had got quite dark and we thought we ought to go back to the room where the disco was held.

I was expecting it to be a bit sad, but the DJ was manic and it turned into quite a rave. All the lads seemed to have forgiven me for my part in the banana-ride ban, and they turned out to be pretty good dancers, too, even if they did have more energy than style.

Around ten o'clock, Karl got hold of my hand and said, 'Cool off outside?'

I nodded, smiling. I wanted to be on my own with him again. We went outside and stood by the pool. There were loads of other couples out there, too, wandering along under the palm trees and snogging on the sunbeds.

Karl looked at me. 'What d'you say, partner? Head for the hills?'

I nodded at him, again, grinning, and without another word we left.

♥

A Friend In Need

It was unreal, packing early next morning to go back. It felt like we were tearing everything down. I could hardly bear the thought that we were leaving the heat and the magic wind, the blue sea and the bluer sky. There was a choking lump in my throat as I crammed my clothes into my suitcase. The only thing that stopped me bursting out crying was knowing Karl would be on the same bus to the airport, and on the same plane home.

Zoë told me she'd had a lovely night with Alexander, and he hadn't pressured her at all. She was all full of hope again. They'd exchanged addresses, and he'd promised to come and visit, maybe at Christmas. Christmas. It was so far away it felt like the millennium after next.

Soon we'd handed back the keys and loaded the cases onto the bus. Then we were on our way to Faliraki. When Karl got on the bus I stood up, and bravely walked down towards the front to sit next to him. I was all tensed up, waiting for the lads to start messing around or teasing me, but nothing happened.

Relieved, I laced my fingers into Karl's, and we sat

looking out of the window in silence as the coach drove through Faliraki. Then we were onto a narrow track, with fields either side.

'It's going to be weird not seeing cacti growing everywhere,' I murmured.

'Or goats.'

'Or . . .' I broke off. Just ahead of us, on his bike, was the unmistakably glamorous form of Alexander. And behind him, hugged in close, was a girl with long dark hair. She was leaning up against his back, face pressed against his shirt, eyes closed in pleasure.

'Oh, no,' I murmured.

'It could be just a friend,' said Karl, doubtfully.

'No it couldn't,' I replied. I recognised that way of sitting on the back of a bike.

Slowly, I turned my head to Zoë, to see if she'd seen. She had. She looked stricken. She looked as though someone had dealt her a death blow.

The bus pulled out past Alexander and his new girl-friend, and overtook them. I didn't know what to do. I looked round again, but Zoë wouldn't meet my eyes. I got this feeling she didn't want me to join her. Her face was frozen; I knew she was fighting for self control.

At the airport, I had a real battle with myself. Zoë was going through the motions like an automaton, but I knew she needed me. And all I wanted to do was be with Karl.

'You didn't hesitate to drop me when Alexander came along, did you?' I muttered under my breath. 'And now you expect me to drop Karl to comfort you. Well, too bad.'

But as I looked at her stricken face, I knew I had no choice. Zoë had been totally smitten: she'd dropped me because she couldn't help herself. That was part of the problem. That was why she was suffering so much now.

Karl came up beside me and put a lovely, warm arm round my shoulders. 'I've checked with the steward,' he said. 'There's a free seat in our row.'

'Is there? Oh, Karl . . .'

'Come and sit with me,' he said, persuasively. 'Come on. It'll make leaving Greece not seem so bad if you're next to me.'

I twisted round and buried my face in his neck. I breathed in his scent; I looked up at his jaw, his mouth. Temptation wasn't in it. My finer self knew I should be with Zoë, while the rest of me just wanted to snuggle up with Karl. They fought an all-out battle for a few seconds and then – a bit to my surprise – my finer self won.

'Karl,' I said, looking straight at him. 'Zoë needs me right now. I mean she *really* needs me.'

And to his everlasting credit, he nodded in agreement. 'I guess she does,' he said, stroking my hair back. 'You're a great friend to her.'

'Reckon she appreciates it?' I said, a bit ruefully.

'I appreciate it,' he said.

Melt? You could have mopped me up with a J cloth.

When we got on the plane, I went and sat beside Zoë. After half an hour's choked silence and two glasses of white wine, the hurt began to pour out. I let her talk

and talk. She sounded totally lost, totally betrayed –
the way she saw it, she just hadn't been great enough to
hold Alexander's interest. I couldn't bear the way she
spoke, as though she was stupid, a dupe, a failure, and
everything that had happened had just been a sham,
fake, worthless.

'Look,' I said, drawing a deep breath, 'it wasn't all
a sham. It *wasn't*. Nothing can take away from you
that you *felt* that way, right? I mean, what you felt
was *real*. And incredible. And if you have real feelings
– you can't avoid hurt sometimes. That creep was just
playing stupid games and cheating. He's obviously
incapable of *real* feeling. You know something? I
wouldn't want *his* emotional life. I feel quite sorry
for him.'

Boy, was I inspired or what? Zoë was drinking in
every word I said, as though I had a potion that would
cure her.

'He's the real loser, Zoë, not you,' I went on,
scornfully. 'What you felt was *real* – what he felt
was just – I mean, he's fake. He's sad. You do know
this wasn't about not sleeping with him, don't you?
You know this would have happened even if you *had*
slept with him? I mean – he's that type of guy. He
makes the beach vampires look like beginners. He's a
professional fake, and if you fake things, you end up
with a fake life. Whereas *you* – you'll meet someone
soon who'll feel as strongly about you as you did
about him. You'll end up with something real. I know
you will.'

Zoë gave a long shuddering sigh, and laid back on

the head rest. 'Oh, Bri,' she said. 'I was such a cow to you. I spoilt your holiday. I just went . . .'

'Mental,' I said soothingly. 'And it's OK.'

Then Zoë had another little cry and within five minutes, she'd fallen into an exhausted sleep.

I stood up and walked to the back of the plane, where Karl and the boys were spreadeagled. Mike, the blond guy, and Karl had a row to themselves. Mike was asleep in the outside seat. Beyond that, was Karl, sprawled and gorgeous. And on the other side of him, a space. My space. He'd saved me the window seat.

I didn't hang about. After all, I was an old hand at this seat-hopping lark. I climbed over Mike, balancing with incredible skill on the chair arms, and landed right in Karl's lap.

The rest of the flight was fantastic.

Not The End

Getting home was so strange. It felt alien, somehow.
It was as though I'd been away for a lot, lot longer
than two weeks. I gave everyone the presents I'd
bought them and the two postcards I'd forgotten
to post. Then I told them a bit about the holiday,
how great it had been, while they admired my tan
and the sun-bleached streaks in my hair. I didn't
mention Karl. Not yet. Somehow, in the grey light
of England, it didn't feel quite real.

After an hour or so I went upstairs and lay on my
bed. I felt drained, and a bit wobbly – almost as if
everything that had happened had been fantasy. I
twisted the silver bracelet round and round on my
wrist, and I missed Karl so badly it made my throat
ache. After a while I fell asleep.

When I woke up it was getting dark, and Mum was
tapping on my bedroom door. 'Brianna?' she called
softly. 'Are you awake?'

'Yeah – yeah I am,' I said, yawning.

'There's a young man here to see you. He says he's
ridden all the way from . . .' I heard her turn away
and call down the stairs –

'*Where* did you say you'd come from?'